THE GANGSTER'S PRIZE

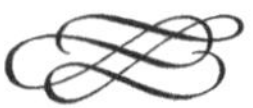

JOANNA SHUPE

CHAPTER 1

New York City, 1890
Tenth Avenue Athletic Club

Isabelle

I came dressed like death.

Wearing my aunt's old widow's weeds, I slipped inside the club and began threading through the raucous crowd. My stomach was cramped with nerves, but I pressed on. The devil was here somewhere. Billy Baxter, leader of the Hell's Kitchen Gang.

The entire city lived in terror of this man. But I hadn't the luxury of terror, not any longer. My father was missing and I had to find him.

My father had recently finished an eight-year term as New York City's comptroller, where he cracked down on corruption and graft. He was a hero in this city. The newspapers had even dubbed him "Honest" Dan Kelly.

Not everyone appreciated his crusade, however. Some viewed my father as an enemy and threatened his life. Now he was missing . . . and all evidence pointed to Mr. Baxter as the responsible party.

So I needed to find the notorious gang leader tonight and force him to talk to me.

Unfortunately, Mr. Baxter was never alone in public. He went everywhere with a bevy of women at his side, along with several members of his gang. No stranger drew within ten feet of the man, not if they wished to live. So I searched while keeping the black veil over my face, a harmless widow in the crowd.

The place was packed with loud men and scantily clad women. They were laughing and cheering, drinking and kissing. It was a world unlike anything I'd imagined. Free and exciting, and without the rules and expectations that weighted down my life. Here, no one paid me any attention.

My eyes drifted to the front row. A man sat there with four well-dressed women draped over him like fine silk. Men nodded in deference as they passed, as if paying homage to a king.

Was this Mr. Baxter?

I tugged on the sleeve of the older fellow next to me. "Pardon me, sir. That man over there with the women. Who is he?"

His brow creased in concern. "Oh, you don't want nothing to do with Billy Baxter, ma'am. Stay far, far away from the likes of him."

So, it was Mr. Baxter. Based on the rumors about him, I'd expected scars and menace. A rough and hulking figure in bloodstained clothes.

He was nothing of the sort.

He was handsome, with a chiseled jaw and lean patrician features. Rather a large nose, but it suited him. His dark hair was swept back to reveal the hint of a widow's peak. His appearance reminded me of the statues of Roman emperors in the history museum. Strong, fearsome. A warrior of old.

He wore a fine navy suit, his keen gaze on the ring. Occasionally he whispered to the woman directly on his right as she stroked his thigh affectionately. Though he was relaxed, danger crackled in the air around him.

Well, dangerous or not, he needed to answer my questions. I had to find my father.

Papa was the only relative I had left. Without him I had no one. And there was no time to lose. Each minute he was gone meant more danger, more risk.

Suddenly, the contest in the ring took a turn and the crowd swelled, growing excited as people yelled and jeered at the fighters. The melee gave me the opportunity to weave unnoticed through the sweaty bodies and move closer to Mr. Baxter.

I edged around the spectators and reached the corner of the ring. The path to him was clear, as if no one dared get too close. Taking a deep breath for courage, I threw my shoulders back and marched forward.

As if he sensed my arrival, his head snapped toward me. His face revealed nothing, however, as he tracked my progress with a cool, dispassionate expression. My heart raced, every instinct screaming for me to turn and run away, yet I soldiered on. Had I any other choice?

When I was a short distance away, I withdrew a pistol from my skirts. I pointed it directly at Mr. Baxter's face.

My hand trembled slightly, but I didn't move. A hush rippled over the crowd until the entire space became quieter than a tomb. Mr. Baxter held my stare, his dark gaze flat and curious, but remained silent.

The men behind him withdrew their pistols and cocked the hammers, but Mr. Baxter held up a hand to wave them off. "Everyone out. Now."

The command was quiet, laced with the rough edges of downtown. The crowd reacted as if he'd shouted. People scattered and chairs overturned. Shouts of "Hurry! Go! Move it!" echoed in the large space.

Mr. Baxter's women hung back until he added, "I said everyone."

The women shot wary glances my way, but I hardly noticed. My focus remained fixed on the man in front of me. He leaned over and whispered to the woman on his right. Nodding, she rose and led the rest of the females away.

Then we were alone.

Mr. Baxter gestured to the empty room. "You have my attention, widow. I assume you're not here to kill me, else you'd already have pulled the trigger. Why don't you show me your face, yeah?"

Reaching with one hand, I shoved the heavy netting up until it fell down my back like a lace waterfall. My unobstructed gaze met his—and I suddenly couldn't breathe. The intense weight of his dark stare went through me, my lungs squeezing tight. I lifted my chin and tried to remain calm. Something told me this man fed on fear.

The edges of his mouth curled. "Well, well. The fancy daughter of a politician at a Tenth Avenue boxing match."

I nearly dropped the gun. "You know who I am."

"You are Miss Isabelle Kelly, the only child of Honest Dan Kelly, current mayoral candidate and former city comptroller."

I clasped the gun with both hands, steadying my aim. "Now perhaps you'll explain why you kidnapped him."

Mr. Baxter rose and straightened his cuffs. "Not many would dare to accuse me of such a deed to my face, let alone hold me at gunpoint." He approached with slow, measured steps, and sweat broke out between my shoulder blades. He looked me up and down. "Lucky for you, I don't offend easily—at least when the offense comes from a beautiful woman."

Up close, Mr. Baxter was even more intriguing. Indeed, more handsome. The navy wool suit fit him perfectly, the simple cloth well-tailored and clean. His dark eyes swirled with intelligence and gleamed with perspicacity, as if the game had already been waged and won in his mind. He was clean shaven, but the hint of whiskers kissed his square jaw.

I wouldn't be fooled, though. This man was dangerous, a criminal, and had probably kidnapped my father.

Despite my trembling hands, I kept the barrel of the gun pointed at him. "Do you claim ignorance, Mr. Baxter?"

"Call me Bax." He leaned a hip against the ring's platform and folded his arms. "And kidnapped, you say? Tell me why I'm responsible."

"Three days ago, my father disappeared from our home, the latch on a downstairs window pried open with a metal tool, his office in shambles. The only clue was a piece of paper from the American Ice Company—your ice company."

"You believe this implicates me."

"Yes, I do."

"It could mean your father purchased ice from my company."

"I review all the household bills. We have never purchased ice—or anything else—from you. That piece of paper was dropped by the kidnappers."

"What do the coppers say? I assume you talked to them."

His smug attitude scraped across my nerves like the tines of a fork. "They lost interest when they saw the name of your company on that piece of paper."

Bax lifted his hands and shrugged. "No one ever claimed the Metropolitan Police were efficient—unless we're talking about accepting bribes. Then there are none more expeditious. What do you want from me, Miss Kelly?"

"Did you kidnap my father?"

"No."

The response came quickly. Almost too quickly. "Why should I believe you?"

"If I kidnapped him, there'd be no reason to hide it. Do you honestly think anyone in this city would lift a finger to stop me from doing whatever I wanted?"

No, I didn't. "Perhaps one of your men kidnapped him without your knowledge."

"My men don't eat, shit or fuck without my permission, let alone kidnap someone, widow. And why would I bother kidnapping your father?"

"My father is running for mayor this autumn on a reform platform. No doubt your livelihood would have suffered under such reforms."

"You think I'm scared of your father?" He snorted and lifted his chin. "I'm above the law, Miss Kelly. Untouchable. A king below

Fiftieth Street. I see these so-called reforms for what they are: hot air from men who like to hear themselves talk. Now, get that gun out of my face so we can have a real conversation, yeah?"

I believed him. There was no artifice, no hesitation in his voice. My shoulders sagged and I lowered the gun. Blast it all. I honestly thought Billy Baxter held the key to my father's whereabouts. Without that lead, what did I have?

Absolutely nothing.

This was a waste of time. I needed to return to police headquarters and press them to investigate. Perhaps if I told them of Mr. Baxter's denial, they would reconsider. I shoved the gun back in my pocket and turned for the door. "Thank you for your time, sir. I'm truly sorry to have bothered you."

"Wait."

The single word was laced with command and I immediately stopped. Bax came to stand in front of me, the lines of his face sharper. More determined. "Do you honestly believe you can stroll in here, hold a gun on me in front of a crowd, then turn around and walk out?"

My throat nearly closed in terror, but I tried to brave it out. "I already apologized."

"We have a different way of settling things around here."

"And what is your way of settling things?"

He rubbed a hand along his jaw as he stared down at me. I couldn't tell what he was thinking. "What're you planning to do about your father?"

"I haven't any idea." Hopelessness, hollow and painful, twisted in my belly. "Hire Pinkertons, I suppose. I know he's alive. If they wanted him dead, they would've killed him in his study. Why bother to take him from his home?"

"Pinkertons are a waste of time and money."

"I haven't any other choice. The police won't help."

"I'll help you."

I blinked at him, certain I'd heard incorrectly. "You would help me?"

"I might be convinced to do so, yeah."

"Meaning?"

"Meaning I won't involve myself out of the kindness of my heart."

This I believed. It was rumored he had no kindness. "I can't pay you, not right away. But my father—"

"It's not money I'm after, widow."

The words bounced off the walls. I froze as the room narrowed down to only the two of us. His expression turned positively predatory, and I prayed my instincts were wrong, that he didn't want the one thing girls were warned about. "What are you after, sir?"

"That's the wrong question to ask."

"Then what is the right question?"

"What're you willing to do for me, Miss Kelly? How far are you willing to go to find out what happened to your father?"

CHAPTER 2

Baxter

*W*ell, well. The night was certainly looking up.

I returned to my chair and let her absorb the words. Once there I busied myself with a cigarette, but it was damn hard to employ patience.

Did she remember me? While it had been a long time ago, I hadn't forgotten her face. How could I, when she was the most beautiful thing a sixteen-year-old boy had ever clapped eyes on in his miserable life?

When we were still rising in the ranks, the boys and I used to go to the Seventh Avenue Mission for the occasional meal. We'd take the food outside, where we could eat in peace.

One night a man was there, giving a speech about the scourge of gangs and violence. He was Daniel Kelly, New York City's new comptroller, and he promised to help crack down on crime in the city. It pissed me and the boys off, especially when he pointed and called us "vermin."

"We ain't fucking vermin," Timmy said on my right. "He's the fucking vermin."

"Fuck him," Jack added from my other side.

There was a dead rat not even two feet away. "Maybe he don't know what vermin is," I said. "Maybe we should put that rat in his carriage. That'd show him."

"Do it." Jack elbowed me. "He'll piss his proper pants."

I found a flat piece of metal and scooped up the rat. Edging around the crowd, I approached the fancy carriage. I started to lean in the window—and found her sitting inside. The prettiest girl I'd ever come across.

I couldn't move, awestruck by her delicate features and dazzling smile.

"Hello," she said to me.

I dropped the dead rodent. My mouth wouldn't work, so I stood there. Staring. I hadn't seen that color hair before. It looked like spun gold in the gaslight. Her skin glowed with health and happiness. She was an angel.

The crowd began clapping. The girl nodded toward the street. "You better go. My father's coming."

My legs carried me back to the boys. When I sat, they clapped me on the shoulder. Timmy said, "I can't wait to hear him scream when he spots that rat!"

"I didn't do it." I couldn't defile the carriage, not with an angel sitting in it. "Don't worry. We'll come up with another way to get back at Daniel Kelly."

I had watched that night as Kelly climbed into the carriage. The girl gazed at him like a diamond necklace and slice of roast beef rolled into one. But he spared not a single glance for her. Instead, he'd shoved her aside to wave out of the carriage window, his smile slick.

Some do-gooder. Treating his own daughter like dirt so he could soak up the attention and praise of strangers.

In a snap, I hated Daniel Kelly.

As I smoked, I regarded Isabelle. I hadn't thought of her much after that night. After all, she was the unattainable princess, too good for a rotten man like me.

But all these years later, the angel was here in my club. And she was even more beautiful, with all the curves I loved on a woman.

Better, she needed help.

I really was a bastard, because I couldn't resist turning the situation to my advantage. It was what I did best, after all.

"What will I do? How far will I go?" The edges of her mouth turned down. "What does that mean?"

"Exactly what I said. Tell me what you're offering."

"What do you want? Money?"

Now we were getting somewhere. I blew out a stream of smoke. "Perhaps it's to merely spend time with you."

"Doing what?"

I threw my head back and laughed. Was she truly this innocent? If so, it hardly made this fun. I had no interest in taking a woman against her will. And seducing a sheltered uptown princess—even the daughter of a man I hated—sounded boring as fuck.

I liked my women eager. Experienced. Filthy.

Not that I'd had time for any recently. Being king of the underworld consumed my every minute. There truly was no rest for the wicked.

"Forget it," I said, pushing to my feet and putting out my cigarette. "Run along, Miss Kelly. Good luck with your Pinkertons. They'll never find your father."

I shoved my hands in my trouser pockets and started for the exit. There was a meeting in a few minutes down at the docks and I needed—

"Wait!"

Miss Kelly's hand landed on my arm, and I swore I could feel the heat from her body through layers of cloth. Awareness crawled over my skin. It caused my voice to come out sharper than I intended when I asked, "What is it, Miss Kelly?"

"Please, wait. I really do need your help."

"Yeah? So what are you willing to give me? And before you answer, let me warn you. It had better be worth it. I'm a busy man, yeah?"

Seconds dragged and she hesitated. I took pity on her. "You're too innocent for the likes of these games, Miss Kelly. Go back uptown, where you and your precious hymen belong. Leave the dirty business to men like me."

Her lips pressed flat and something flashed in her expression. Determination? Anger? "I'm not as innocent as I appear."

It took everything I had not to laugh. Instead, I dropped back a step and folded my arms. "Yeah? Prove it."

Would she tell me a tedious tale about sharing sloppy kisses with the groom's son? Or how she'd once read a racy novel? I resisted the urge to check my pocket watch for the time. I didn't want to be late for this meeting.

She stared at the floor. Just when I lost all hope, she reached for her skirts. With shaking hands, she began lifting them.

I froze. What the hell?

A better man would've stopped her, but I was not about to interrupt whatever was happening. Was she about to flash me her quim?

No, impossible. Honest Dan Kelly's daughter would never—

Then I saw a flash of red silk and white lace. My mouth went dry. Those were her drawers? I would've expected burlap or the thickest cotton known to man. Padlocked and sewn shut.

But this . . . ? Jesus fuck.

Her calves were wrapped in white silk stockings. Red silk clung to her thighs, and a delicate edge of white lace peeked out below her knees. I sucked in a breath. Heat blasted through me like a furnace, settling low in my belly.

They were the most erotic drawers I'd ever seen.

And they were on an uptown virgin?

"How . . .?" It was the best I could manage, considering.

"I have a collection. They make me feel confident. Pretty."

She started to drop her skirts, so I had to intervene. "No, wait. Just a few more seconds, now that I've recovered from the shock."

"I feel silly," she whispered, but kept her lower half exposed to my greedy gaze.

Her thighs were thick and perfect, exactly the kind a man liked to sink between to lose himself. I couldn't see her pussy, but I wondered if this little show was turning her on. Was she wet? My cock twitched at the idea. I would love nothing more than to drop to this hard floor, shove my face in her folds, and tongue her until she screamed. "You little vixen."

Her fingers opened and the skirts fell to her toes. "So you see, you were wrong about me. Now, will you help me find my father?"

I stroked my jaw and considered this. My dick had a clear opinion on the matter, but I hadn't let him run me around since I was a lad. No, I had to think about this logically.

Not many people surprised me, and the little widow had gone and done it twice tonight. Maybe I was wrong about her being boring and sheltered. Maybe she had a naughty streak just waiting to be fanned like the spark of a flame.

And her father would fucking hate her being associated with the likes of me.

I ran my tongue over my teeth. "Does the corset match?"

"Of course—but I'm not showing you."

I could demand it, but I really did need to leave for my meeting. I went with my gut, which was never wrong, and made a decision.

I started for her. She tracked my approach, her big eyes shining up at me. Frightened or excited? Maybe both? *Christ*, I couldn't wait to find out.

She began backing up, but the ring prevented her escape. Instead of going for her gun again, she lifted her chin and stood her ground. *Good girl.*

Closer now, I could see the bluish veins under her pale skin, the beat of her pulse along her throat. Leaning in, I dragged a knuckle over her smooth jaw. It felt like the purest silk. I longed to run my lips over that soft expanse, then scrape it with my teeth. "You agree to do whatever I want, widow, whenever I want it."

Her breath hitched. "No," she whispered. "I couldn't possibly."

I let that statement linger as my finger trailed down the heavy fabric covering her throat. Her pulse fluttered under my touch, but I didn't stop. Instead, I moved lower, along the fine arch of her collarbone, then across to her shoulder. She was dainty and feminine, but strong. The perfect combination in a woman.

"Do you want help with finding your father?" I asked softly.

"Yes, but I won't sleep with you."

I caressed her arm, my fingertips grazing her elbow, and she shivered. "You will—and you'll beg me for it."

"You're delusional."

I stepped back, smothering a smile. "So what will it be? Am I saving Honest Dan Kelly for you?"

"Do you agree with me that he's still alive?"

"Yes, because it would be stupid to kill such a high-profile figure and think to get away with it. They are clearly waiting to ransom him off."

She seemed to mull this over. "Can you get him released quickly?"

"Hard to say. It will take time." Days and days, if it meant keeping her by my side. Weeks, maybe. Hell, I might wait until next year.

"I don't want him suffering in some damp warehouse or musty opium den until you do."

"I'll see that he's well cared for by his kidnappers—if you play nice."

"So you know his whereabouts."

"My reach in this city is vast and pervasive. I have the ability to ensure his well being, if I choose to involve myself. Am I involving myself?"

I didn't miss the way her gaze flicked over my body, then traveled up to my mouth. Lust raced through me, my skin prickling with awareness. She was curious, I could tell. Wondering how it would be between us.

I'd make it so good for you, angel.

She closed her eyes. "Fine. I'll let you kiss me."

"Such a sacrifice," I murmured. "And you have it backwards, yeah? It's whatever *I* want, not whatever *you* want."

"Too vague. I won't agree to a deal without knowing the terms first. Nor, I suspect, would you."

She was so cute. Did she honestly think to negotiate with me? "The clock is ticking, widow."

"What you are suggesting will ruin my reputation."

"A woman with drawers like yours?" I smirked. "I'd wager she isn't worried about her reputation."

She bit her bottom lip, and I watched the plump flesh disappear between her teeth. Envy crawled through my veins. I wanted to bite her, then have her bite me in return. This was going to be fun.

"For how long?" she asked, her voice thin.

"As long as it takes."

"To get him released?"

"Among other things," I said cryptically.

"I don't really have a choice, do I?"

"You're asking a lot of questions for a woman who very nearly showed me her quim two minutes ago. I told you what I want. Are you in or out?"

"I'm in."

A dark thrill unfurled in my stomach, moving lower to my groin. "Good. Follow me."

CHAPTER 3

Isabelle

This was madness.

I was letting Billy Baxter lead me outside of the club toward the street. I had no idea where we were going and my father was still missing.

So why was my heart beating so fast in my chest?

Now Bax knew my secret obsession with fancy French undergarments, the delicate, racy sort unavailable in America. This happened to be one of my favorite sets, red silk with white lace on each leg. Tiny beads in the lace shimmered in the light. I felt powerful and bold in these garments, which was precisely why I'd worn them this evening.

"You little vixen."

I knew the ensemble was pretty, but Baxter's reaction made me feel like the most gorgeous woman in the city. No one had ever regarded me so carefully and with such admiration. My father usually ignored me or treated me like I was an annoyance.

As if Bax could read my mind, he asked, "Does your father know you own such undergarments?"

"Good heavens, of course not." Papa didn't pay much attention to anything when it came to me. He was more concerned with his career and speeches.

"I am busy at the moment, Isabelle."

"I haven't any time for this, Isabelle."

"You couldn't possibly understand, Isabelle."

But he was all I had. My only family, my rock. Yes, his causes came first, but I couldn't complain. His hard work was making a difference for the people of New York.

I used to grow angry when he insisted that I refuse my invitations and stay home. But now that all my friends from finishing school had married, what would I do? They were much too busy with their own lives to spare me any time.

So the undergarments became my naughty secret. I got a thrill every time I put on one of the pieces. I felt less bored and pathetic in them. And in addition to what I owned, I had pages and pages of designs that I'd drawn. Patterns I dreamed of one day seeing produced for women to wear.

It was silly. My father would never allow such a scandalous enterprise, nor would a husband. No, my existence would continue to be dictated by the men in my life, while I waited at home, over and over until I died.

A depressing thought, but then women in my world weren't bred for exciting lives. We were praised for our chastity and the ability to keep a man's home. Which most days felt dashed unfair.

"What about the staff?" Bax asked.

"My maid is the only one who knows and she would never betray my trust. What I wear under my clothing is no one's concern but my own."

"And mine."

"For now."

A big hand wrapped around my upper arm and pulled me to a stop. Bax's body was right there, pressed close to mine, and his heat sank under my skin. He put his mouth near my ear. "As long as you're with me, I'm the only man to see those undergarments. If you show them to anyone else, he won't live to draw another breath."

The violence should have repelled me. This man was a hooligan, a killer. I should run far, far away from him.

Yet the rough threat excited me, and I swayed closer to his large frame. He smelled of tobacco, leather and gunpowder, and I had the strangest desire to press my lips to his.

Goodness, what was I doing? I could already hear my father's disappointment. *"People will only take advantage of you. You're better off staying at home, Isabelle."*

I needed to keep my wits about me. This was to save my father. Nothing more.

"I have no intention of showing my undergarments to anyone," I said.

Bax nodded. "Good girl. Let's get in the carriage. I have a meeting a few blocks away, but it won't take long."

"A meeting?"

"Yeah, a meeting. I told you I was busy. Have patience."

Patience? Was he serious?

My father was missing. God only knew what the kidnappers were doing to him. And Bax wanted me to have patience? The tips of my ears grew hot and I pressed my lips together to keep from screeching at him.

We approached a black closed carriage with matching curtains. If it were a tad longer, the conveyance could have passed for a funeral carriage.

Death. It looks like death.

Appropriate considering how I was dressed. Still, apprehension crawled over the nape of my neck like tiny spiders. Was I really going along with him? And where would he go after the meeting, a robbery? A saloon? A *brothel?*

Any sane woman would have refused this bargain. But I was desperate. I needed my only family to safely return home.

For that, I could put up with the devil and his underworld kingdom for a few nights.

A young boy jumped down to open the door. He was likely only nine or ten. He offered no word in greeting, just stood as still as a statue.

"The docks, Pete," Bax said he handed me up.

Bax sat next to me, his large frame overwhelming in such a cramped space. I hadn't been this close to a strange man before. I tried to edge away, but there wasn't anywhere to go.

"You best get used to it," he said. "We'll be getting very close, Belle."

A nickname? No one had given me one before, not even the girls at finishing school. I wanted to protest, but I liked it. It felt special, a thing just between us.

"What is this meeting about?" I asked, desperate for anything that would take my mind off the heavy weight of his thigh against mine.

"Are you genuinely interested? Or filling the silence?"

The truth spilled out of my mouth. "The latter, I suppose."

He chuckled. "I like when you're honest."

"Why?"

"Because you lie to everyone all day long, pretending to be one thing when you're really not. I'm much more interested in a woman who goes after what she wants, rather than one who plays it safe."

He couldn't possibly understand my life. "I haven't a choice. There are certain expectations that go along with being the daughter of Honest Dan Kelly."

"Such as?"

"Maintaining my reputation and avoiding scandal. We always had to worry about re-election."

Bax's hand shifted to rest on his big thigh, and his pinky finger was dangerously close to my leg. I couldn't stop staring at the digit, wondering if he would touch me. What would it feel like, rough or soft?

"What other expectations are there?"

Glancing away from his hand, I exhaled shakily. "Let's see. Since I returned from finishing school, he prefers me to stay home. He chooses my suitors. And he works long hours, so it's my responsibility to run the house."

"That's no way to live, Belle."

How could I make him understand? This man could do what he liked, go where he liked. There was no more powerful criminal in Manhattan. My life was the complete opposite in every way. "I can't complain when I've been given so much. It wouldn't be fair."

"Fair?" He shifted toward me slightly. There was an edge to his voice, one I hadn't heard yet tonight. "No one gives a fuck about fair in this city. Do you think police care about what's fair? What about the residents of those mansions on Fifth Avenue? Or your father? He certainly doesn't care about what's fair."

I studied his face. "How do you know what my father does and does not care about?"

He flicked his fingers. "All politicians are the same."

A sweeping generalization, but I didn't feel like arguing over it. "They say you grew up on the streets."

I nearly winced. Why had I asked such a personal question? This man's life was no concern of mine.

The long pinky finger drifted ever closer. It tapped against his leg, as if impatient to get to me, and I wanted to crawl out of my skin. He had nice hands, strong with veins running along them. Hands that had committed unspeakable violence, no doubt. How would they feel on my body?

"I left home at the age of eight." His deep voice filled the carriage. "Not a unique story, I'm afraid."

"That must've been difficult," I said as his fingers curled into a fist.

"You keep staring at my hand. Is there something you want, widow?"

I jerked my head up and stared straight ahead. "Absolutely not."

"Do you want me to touch you?"

The place between my legs heated and I could feel myself growing wet. "Don't be ridiculous."

"Hmm. Perhaps you'd rather touch me instead?"

Oh, I hadn't considered that. My mouth dried out as I imagined running my hands over his chest and thighs. His groin. The growing bulge in his trousers.

"I'd be so patient with you," he said softly. "I'd teach you how to please me. Show you how good it could be between us."

My eyes drifted to his hand once again. His fingers were slowly trailing up his thick wool-covered thigh toward the center of his legs. I couldn't speak. I couldn't *breathe*.

The placket of his trousers tightened and I could see the stiff column under the cloth. My heart thumped, the pulse echoing between my legs. I wished that was my hand. I wanted to know what a man's erection felt like.

Abruptly, the carriage drew to a halt, interrupting us. I grabbed onto the side to keep myself from pitching forward, both relieved and disappointed the moment was over.

Leaning closer, he murmured, "To be continued."

CHAPTER 4

Baxter

*W*illing my cock to deflate quickly, I jumped out of the carriage and closed the door. "Stay here until I get back."

Belle stared at me with wide eyes. "Wait, you're leaving me?"

"Yeah. Pete'll keep watch. You'll be fine."

While I wanted her with me, I didn't care to truly frighten her. The meeting tonight was not a friendly one. There was every possibility it could turn violent.

I wouldn't risk her safety.

I started toward the warehouse. Matty and the other women trailed me as usual, fingers on their weapons.

Most people assumed my female companions were my lovers. I never corrected the assumption. Why would I, when it kept me safer? Any one of these four women was more deadly than a Bowery street tough crossed with a river pirate. They'd saved my life and protected me for years, and I compensated them handsomely for it.

Charlie, my right-hand man, waited to open the front door. "Evening, Bax."

"Everyone here?"

"Yeah. And no weapons, just as you said." Charlie tipped his cap at someone behind me. "Evening, miss."

What in fucking hell?

I spun and found Belle there, trying to push her way through my guards. "I told you to wait in the carriage."

"I want to come with you." She lifted her chin.

Everything in me recoiled at the idea. I locked eyes with Matty, my friend and head guard. I trusted her opinion the most, but she shrugged. Damn it.

I didn't want to delay this meeting any longer. If Belle wished to see what I did, then who was I to stop her? "Come on, then." With a gentle push, I guided her inside.

"What is this meeting about?" she whispered.

"Not undergarments," I answered dryly. She elbowed me in response and I had to smother a smile. Feisty widow.

Walsh was already here, sitting at a wooden table in the middle of the empty floor. Three of his men stood behind him. "I don't like to be kept waiting," he called as Belle and I approached.

Irritation slid along my skin like hot wax. Walsh was the leader of the Mudlarks, a river gang in New Jersey. We occasionally partnered on jobs, depending on my mood. These days I was tired of Walsh's incessant demands for a bigger piece of the North River pie. This meeting would settle all that.

Eager to get this over with, I led Belle to the other side of the table. Without giving her a chance to argue, I sat and brought her down onto my lap.

I casually rested a hand on her thigh. I liked the weight of her on me. Was she enjoying the feel of the silk drawers pressed to her skin while in this position? "I hear you have complaints."

Walsh jabbed a finger at the tabletop. "The way I see it, things ain't exactly fair."

"Yeah? You think you deserve more?"

"That river belongs to us," Walsh snapped. "The Mudlarks have always worked it alongside your boys. You're making a fortune while we're scrounging for scraps."

My hand itched for a pistol. I'd love to put a bullet through Walsh's heart. "You're lucky that I'm dealing you in at all. It's pure charity; I don't need your help."

"That's horse shit. I ain't no newcomer, Bax. You can't shove me aside."

Wrong. I could do whatever the hell I wanted. Not many had my muscle in Manhattan, and certainly no one in New Jersey could touch me. "Stop making a nuisance of yourself, or consider it a declaration of war."

"You would go to war instead of giving us our rightful percentage?"

I glared down my considerable nose at him, letting him see the truth of my words. "In a fucking heartbeat. So go back to Jersey and keep the fuck quiet."

"This isn't over, Baxter."

"You've wasted my time." I helped Belle to her feet, then rose. "Worse, you've wasted Miss Kelly's time."

"Do not leave, not until we settle this."

I gestured to where my guards had his men surrounded. "There is nothing to be settled, Walsh. You see who holds all the power here. Stay out of my way."

With a firm grip on Belle's hand, I started for the exit. Once outside, we headed toward my carriage.

"I thought my father was inside," she whispered. "That's why I followed you."

Ah. So she hadn't trusted me.

Smart of her.

"I told you I would deal with your problems after this meeting. You need to start believing me."

I handed her into the carriage and waited as Charlie caught up. "No one goes back to New Jersey alive," I told him quietly.

"No problem, Bax."

"Wait!" Belle leaned out of the open door, her face pale. "Bax, no. You cannot have those men killed."

I regarded her carefully, the moment heavy with expectation. Charlie was probably choking on his tongue that someone questioned one of my orders. Normally I wouldn't tolerate it, but Belle was special. "Why not?"

"You can't fault him for trying to do better by his men."

Yes, I certainly fucking could.

I braced an arm on the side of the carriage. "That meeting was an insult. I can't tolerate insults."

"But it doesn't mean you have to kill them."

Oh, my sweet, sweet girl. Better she learned now the type of man I was. "I'm a bad man who does bad things, sweetheart. This ain't no surprise, yeah?"

"Yes, but is it necessary to do this particular bad thing?"

Charlie muttered, "Bax, we need to know what to do."

I kept my eyes locked on Belle. "Why should I spare their miserable lives?"

"Because it's the decent thing to do. Please, Bax."

Begging. I liked it. Just how far would my naughty widow go to save these men? As far as she'd go to save her father?

"Bax," Charlie said impatiently. "They're trying to leave."

I stared directly at her as I ordered, "Lock them in and burn it down."

She gasped. "No, don't! Please. I'll show you the other thing. From earlier. The matching piece."

Her red corset.

My heart thumped hard as I considered it. I wanted to see her slowly disrobe, willingly remove every item of clothing for me until she reached her corset and chemise. Fuck, that was a performance I could savor for hours. But was it worth leaving Walsh alive?

The answer was obvious.

"Let them go," I said.

Charlie knew better than to question me, so he merely nodded.

Just for him, I added under my breath, "The package I have stashed? I need you to fetch it and bring it to Lisette's."

"Now?"

"Yeah. I'll meet you there when I'm finished."

Charlie saluted and hurried off, taking a few of the men with him. I glanced at Matty and the other guards waiting nearby. "I need to see Miss Kelly home."

Matty nodded once, her eyes flat and serious. "We'll follow in a second carriage."

I climbed inside my carriage and shut the door. The dim lighting did nothing to hide Belle's flushed skin.

When I settled on the opposite seat, I gestured to her bodice. "If you think I am too gentlemanly to collect, think again. I want what you promised and I want it now."

She licked her lips. The pulse in her throat pounded beneath her skin, and I longed to put my tongue there, feel that throbbing heat with my mouth. But there was time enough for that later. This was something else entirely.

"I don't have enough room here." She folded her hands in her lap. "It'll have to wait."

"No, no, no. I've paid for my ticket, widow. Therefore, I demand the show. Take off your clothes—and do it slowly."

"But . . ."

"The corset, Belle. No stalling." I stretched my legs, settling in.

Seconds crawled by but neither of us moved. I was more than happy to wait her out. Promises were promises where I came from.

And I knew that, deep down, she really wanted to show me.

The anticipation was goddamn killing me. Honest Dan Kelly's daughter, in my carriage, about to show me her corset. It was almost too good to be true.

Looking down, she removed her gloves one at a time. Then her fingers danced near her neckline, hovering. Nerves, or was the vixen actually teasing me? My muscles tightened, like an animal ready to pounce at a moment's notice. "Are you trying to drive me out of my skull?"

Her eyes sparkled. "Just ensuring you're paying attention, William."

William? My body went hot and cold, a bolt of white-hot lust filling every vein and cell. No one called me William, ever. I was Bax or Billy, occasionally "Monk."

Jesus fuck, this woman.

While I was still reeling, she plucked at the hooks of her black bodice, unfastening them one by one. I stayed quiet, barely blinking, as she worked.

Lower and lower, her fingers kept going, tantalizing me, and my heart thumped louder than the carriage wheels bouncing over cobblestones. The entire city could have burned down and I wouldn't have been able to tear my eyes away from her delicate hands.

When the bodice was undone, she held out her arm. "You'll have to pull."

CHAPTER 5

Isabelle

*W*hy wasn't I nervous? I was removing my clothing in front of a man. Yet the way Bax looked at me made me feel powerful. Beautiful and in control.

He reached for my sleeve and gently pulled to help me slip my arm from the fitted fabric. Cool air washed over my newly revealed skin as I angled to give him my other arm. "Now this one."

He complied silently, acting like the most handsome and dangerous ladies' maid I'd ever encountered. When I was free, I let the bodice fall behind my back and squared my shoulders. Though my arms were now bare, I still wore a thin black cover over my corset for protection.

We turned a corner and the streets grew smoother. Broadway, probably. I was grateful for the heavy curtains that covered the windows. At least no one would ever know I had disrobed in front of the notorious Billy Baxter.

The buttons on the corset cover were tiny and my hands were

trembling, so it was slow going. I tried to keep the sides closed as I opened the garment, just to prolong his torture—and mine. The intense way his eyes tracked my movements caused a slick heat to bloom between my thighs. Did he find this arousing, too? Would the sight of me in such dishabille produce another erection in his trousers? Oh, how I hoped so.

Finally, I peeled off one side and then the other. I let him look his fill at the red corset edged with white satin.

He took his time with his examination. My chest rose and fell quickly with the force of my breaths, and the carriage closed in on us, like we were our own little island. The sweep of his intense gaze caused goose bumps all along my skin.

"My God, Belle," he rasped. "You are stunning."

"Do you like it?"

"If you were anyone else, I'd be fucking you already."

I almost asked why I didn't qualify, but immediately thought better of it. There was no use in provoking him, not when I had no intention of handing over my virtue to him. "You are quite fond of that word."

"Because it has so many practical uses. If you ask nicely, I'll show you my favorite one."

I didn't dare ask. I feared I would like the answer too much.

Reaching for the corset cover, I started to shrug it on. He put up a hand. "Wait. Don't."

"Why?"

"Come here."

The rough order was laced with quiet authority, an undeniable command. I considered refusing but, in truth, I didn't *want* to. Whatever was happening between us pulled at a deep part of me, one I hadn't even known existed. It was the place inside me yearning to be noticed, to be desired. To *matter* to someone else.

And Bax noticed me.

This man, one who commanded half the island of Manhattan, noticed me. Wanted me, even. It seemed unreal, but the truth was plain in the lust stamped across his flushed features.

Still, I hesitated. What did he plan to do?

"Anything I want, whenever I want it." He jerked his chin and patted his thigh. "That's our bargain, widow."

My enthusiasm dimmed considerably. This was a bargain, nothing more. I couldn't forget it. I was doing this to save my father and Bax was doing this to . . . humiliate me? Humiliate my father? Either way, this wasn't a romance, and I was Bax's willing strumpet for however long it took to rescue my father.

I had to remain brave. Sliding across the carriage, I gingerly placed my bottom on Bax's knees. *It's no different than sitting on his lap during the meeting.*

Except the upper half of my body was nearly naked.

His palms swept up my back and across my ribs, shaping and testing me. Feeling how the garment supported my breasts. My nipples tightened inside the whalebone, silk and cotton, pushing out and begging for his attention. *Yes, definitely a strumpet.*

His hands drifted over my middle. "Look at all the beauty you've been hiding under that hideous crepe gown."

"That is generally where undergarments are worn. Under gowns." I was nearly panting, my voice thin from lack of air.

"I wasn't referring to the undergarments."

My belly clenched at the compliment. No one had ever said something so thrilling about me before. "Thank you."

"Is it comfortable?"

"Yes, actually. It's very well constructed. The silk is imported from —" Dash it. Billy Baxter didn't care about the stitching of my expensive undergarment.

"Don't stop," he urged, his fingers gliding perilously close to the mounds of my breasts.

I wanted him to touch me there. Desperately. I arched my back ever so slightly.

"Belle. Keep talking."

"Hmm? Oh, the silk. You don't really wish to hear all that, I'm sure."

"Wrong. I want to hear every thought going on in that gorgeous brain of yours."

He really needed to stop with these compliments. They weren't necessary. "The silk is woven in Lyon by a group of nuns. They've used the same process for hundreds of years, taught to them by the Italians when they first moved into the area. Then the silk is shipped to Maison Joubert in Paris. Monsieur Joubert designs these corsets."

"Yeah? All I know is I fucking like the feel of it."

"I have seven others," I said.

He groaned and dropped his head back onto the seat. "You're killing me, widow."

"I don't care if people think it's extravagant or wasteful. Some Fifth Avenue princess wasting her father's money—"

"Whoa." He slid me closer. "I didn't say any of that. If you want to spend your pin money on pretty undergarments, who am I to complain? I love the way you look in them."

"You don't think they make me look loose?"

"No one could ever accuse you of being loose." He dragged a fingertip along the satin edging, and I shivered. "If they do, they will answer to me—and I will cut their tongues out for disrespecting you."

My heart swelled like a lovesick schoolgirl. Why was that the most romantic thing I'd heard? Goodness, I was being foolish.

I inhaled and reminded myself who I was and who I was with. This was a means to save my father, nothing more. "It doesn't matter, because I can't buy them any longer."

"Why not?"

"The tariffs on luxury fabrics. The customs house charges almost double the cost of garments like this."

His head shot up, eyebrows lowered in curiosity. "What?"

"The law started earlier this year. It's the McKinley Tariff Act. Haven't you heard of it?"

"No. We play by our own rules over in Hell's Kitchen. Besides, laws were made to be broken, Belle."

"Not for me," I rushed to say. "I'm Honest Dan Kelly's daughter."

He opened his mouth then closed it, like he'd thought better of whatever popped into his head. I couldn't leave it alone, so I asked, "What were you going to say?"

"Nothing. No doubt the stupid law will be repealed soon. The Fifth Avenue ladies won't like paying more for their gowns."

I snorted. "Mrs. Astor already went to war with them and gave up. The customs house confiscated two of her Parisian gowns, charging her double the price. So she let them keep the garments."

"Good for her." He ran a finger down the middle of the corset, right over the fastenings. I could feel his hardness growing beneath my bottom. It felt larger than it had looked earlier. Without thinking, I shifted on his lap.

He hissed through his teeth. "Are you trying to get me to unload in my trousers?"

"No." I instantly stiffened. "Though I don't know what that means."

His chest rose and fell. "Have you never seen a man's cock before?"

"Of course not." My skin was on fire, like I was standing in front of a furnace.

"Would you like to? Because you've got my balls aching right now, widow. I'd love to show you what that means."

I bit my lip. I admit, I was curious. As soon as my father was released, my life would go back to lonely hours in the house by myself. Right now, I had the chance for excitement and danger. A way to make memories for cold winter nights ahead.

Bax and I were alone, in the middle of the night. Lost somewhere in a carriage in Manhattan. No one would ever know . . . .

"Yes," I whispered.

Bax lifted me and placed my bottom on the seat beside him. "Fuck, I've never been so happy to hear that one word before." His fingers went to his waist and he quickly began unfastening his trousers. "I can't wait to look at you in that corset while I stroke myself off."

Heart thumping, I watched as the buttons fell open. He wore a thin union suit, but I could see the length of his erection behind it. I couldn't look away.

He popped the undergarment and then I saw it. Smooth skin, wide and long. A flushed cap on the end. He gripped the base to pull it free of his clothing. Heavens, was it supposed to be so big?

"What do you think? Do you like it?" He moved his hand up the thick length until he reached the crown. His body twitched and he groaned. "I'm so hard for you, Belle."

"Does it hurt?" I couldn't imagine having this . . . thing grow between my legs.

"No, it feels fucking amazing."

He pumped his hand up and down a few times, his thighs spreading wider. I could feel his gaze on my breasts, which were pushed high under my corset and chemise. But I continued to watch his hand, mesmerized by how he pulled and twisted, manipulating his own flesh. I clenched my thighs, unbelievably aroused. A steady rhythm throbbed in the button atop my swollen sex, insistent and relentless.

"See how much I want you?" He was breathing hard now. "You've had me worked up since you lifted your skirts earlier."

"Yeah?" I whispered.

His hand picked up speed. "Say my name like that, in that throaty whisper."

"Bax."

It was hardly a sound, but he heard me, letting out a moan as he stroked. Raising his free hand, he held one finger up to me. "Suck my finger into your mouth."

I didn't question why. He was my guide, and I was more than eager to follow him down a sinful path tonight.

I parted my lips. Instead of shoving inside roughly, he dragged his fingertip along the edges of my mouth, tracing me. Then he fed his finger gently onto my tongue. My toes curled at his taste and texture, so different from my own finger.

I liked it. I had a part of this man inside my body.

His nostrils flared. "Suck, Belle."

I drew him deeper, tightening my lips. His dark gaze never left my mouth, and his hand moved faster over his shaft. "Tight and wet, just like I imagine your pussy to be."

I was burning up, lust pounding in my veins. The carriage bounced and rocked, but I hardly noticed. I only wished to please him, to see where all this feverish desire led.

A pearl of moisture beaded from the slit on his crown. He used it, smearing the liquid on his shaft. What did that fluid taste like?

When I flicked his finger with my tongue, he groaned. "Oh, shit. It's too much." His chest heaved. "Get the handkerchief out of my inside coat pocket."

Keeping his finger in my mouth, I reached for the pocket and found the soft handkerchief. I held it up for him, but he shook his head. "I'm going to come. Put that cloth over the crown. Catch my spend in it."

The words were tight, rushed. As if there was no time to lose.

I held the handkerchief atop his shaft. He snarled as his hips jerked, and jets of white fluid shot from his body and into the cloth. It went on and on, pulses of hot liquid, and I tried to catch what I could. There was quite a lot of it, and he wasn't exactly remaining still.

When he finally slumped against the seat, his face was relaxed. Almost happy. The hard edge that accompanied him wherever he went had melted away in those few seconds of pleasure. Goodness, he was beautiful.

I looked down. His appendage had deflated. The skin was red, and it glistened with his fluids. Remarkable.

"Less impressive now," he said with a chuckle.

"Less intimidating, as well."

He took the handkerchief from me and wiped his hands off. Then he dropped the used cloth onto the carriage floor. As he refastened his clothing, he asked, "Are you shocked?"

"No."

His head came up and he smirked. "Aroused?"

I couldn't answer. I was aroused, of course, but it wasn't the sort of thing a lady admitted out loud.

"I see. Your pussy making a lot of cream for me?"

The filthy words were unlike anything I'd heard before tonight. I wasn't used to it. "I suppose my drawers are ruined."

The edge of his mouth hitched as he finished with his trousers. "You tell me how to replace them, and I'll have five new pairs delivered as quickly as I can."

"You can't get them."

He leaned over and tucked a strand of hair behind my ear. "I can get anything you want. When you're with me, the world is yours, sweetheart."

The carriage wheels slowed and Bax's brow furrowed. "Damn it."

I took the opportunity to scramble to the other seat. With shaking hands, I started putting myself back to rights.

"Here. Let me help." Bax knelt on the carriage floor and pushed my hands away. He maneuvered the tiny buttons of the corset cover easily.

Then he helped me pull on the bodice and secured each hook, one by one. Occasionally, the back of his hand brushed the mounds of my breasts and my belly tightened with need. I wanted to feel his big hands on me, shaping and molding the sensitive flesh, pinching my nipples . . . all the things I did to myself in the dark.

I whimpered.

Bax's head shot up and his coffee-colored gaze pierced into mine. I bit my lip, mortified.

"Fuck, Belle," he whispered. "The filthy things I want to do to you."

I didn't know what to say. I wanted things as well, but they were much too vague to put into words. My body had demands I didn't understand, needs I barely recognized.

I knew Bax was the key, though. This gang leader had unlocked some secret part of me, and I wasn't certain I wanted to close it back up just yet.

He threw open the carriage door and helped me down. We were parked directly in front of my home on East Sixty-Eighth Street.

Bax started up the walk and I instantly dug in my heels. I couldn't have the neighbors see Billy Baxter escorting me to my door, especially at night. One never knew who could be peeking out their window. "This isn't necessary. It's perfectly safe here."

He slipped on his derby and tugged me toward the stoop. "You're mine for the foreseeable future, Belle. I take care of what is mine."

The possessive words sent a riot of flutters through my belly. I lost my will to fight him and went along to the door.

Once there, he held out a hand. "Key."

I dug into my small bag and retrieved the house key. I held it, not handing it over. "Do you think I'm safe here? After they took my father, I mean."

He lifted the heavy metal piece from my fingers. "I can have a few of the boys come and watch your house at night, if you're worried."

"Bax, you don't need—"

"Belle," he said, his voice tight with impatience. "If it helps you rest easier, then I'll do whatever it takes."

The flutters expanded behind my breastbone. From dressing me in the carriage and now sending his men to stand guard, Bax was certainly looking out for me. "Thank you."

"You're welcome. But fair warning—if I think you're at risk here, I won't hesitate to make you stay elsewhere. Understand?"

I plucked the key back from his hand and swiftly unlocked the door. "I'm sure that won't be necessary. You're going to help me get my father back."

"As long as you keep doing what I want, yeah?"

"I already gave you what you wanted."

"Hardly. In fact, I've now thought of something else I want." He crowded closer. "Do you touch yourself? Between your legs, I mean."

"That is a very personal question." The words came out breathy and surprised rather than annoyed.

"Yeah, it is. What's the answer?"

I considered stalling, but there was no point. I'd agreed to play his game in exchange for my father's rescue. "Yes. Happy that you've embarrassed me?"

He closed his eyes, as if in pain. "Jesus, I'm getting hard again just imagining it." He looked at me intensely. "Listen carefully. Once inside, I want you to go to your room, remove all your clothing and slide into bed completely naked—"

I inhaled sharply. "I couldn't possibly—"

"I'm not finished." He set his hands on my shoulders, keeping me in place. "Once in bed, put your hand between your legs. Pet your pussy with your fingers. Tweak your nipples and cup your breasts.

Rub your clit. I want you to imagine it's me the entire time, that it's my hand giving you pleasure. Keep at it until you climax. Can you do that for me?"

I should've been scandalized by such an order. How could he discuss these things so openly, so frankly? What if someone overhead him?

But part of me liked it. No one spoke to me like this. Yet Bax did.

Bax talked to me as if I were a real person, with thoughts and opinions of my own. Could I do what he was asking?

If it meant pleasing him, then I knew the answer. "Yes."

"Good girl. I'll see you tomorrow afternoon." He jerked his chin in the direction of the door.

"Wait, what about tomorrow? Where am I meeting you?"

"Don't worry. I'll find you." With that, Bax opened my door and guided me inside. "Sweet dreams, widow."

When I was finally inside, I didn't hesitate to hurry upstairs and follow his instructions to the letter.

* * *

Baxter

AFTER GIVING PETE DIRECTIONS, I climbed back into my carriage. Matty was waiting inside. She said, "It smells like sex in here."

Ignoring her, I dug into my coat pocket and pulled out my cigarette case.

That resulted in a sigh. "I hope you know what you're doing."

Matty and I grew up on the streets together, our lives intertwined for what felt like forever now. Lovers once, but not for a long time. Instead, she watched my back along with the other guards, and I trusted her opinion. She was fierce and loyal, and one of the smartest people I knew.

She was also one of the few people to whom I ever explained myself.

"I do." I knocked on the roof and called out, "To Lisette's."

Matty snatched the cigarette out of my fingers and brought it to her lips. "Your little bird put you in the mood for more pussy tonight?"

As if I'd want another woman with the image of Belle sucking my finger still tattooed on my brain. "No. I asked Charlie to bring that package over to Lisette's bordello for safe keeping."

Her eyes rounded. "You're joking." When I lifted an irritated eyebrow, she started laughing. "She really has a hold on you, doesn't she?"

"Fuck off, Matilda." She hated when I used her given name. "I made a promise and I mean to see it through."

"If you want to fuck her, then do it already. There's no reason to drag it out."

"It doesn't work that way," I said. "She's innocent. Well bred. She's only interested in saving her dear old dad."

"Too bad she doesn't know he isn't worth saving."

We were in agreement on that. "I want eyes on her house."

"Why the fuck would we bother?"

"Because I want her kept safe."

"She's in no danger, Bax. Unless it's from you."

I struck a match and held it up to my fresh cigarette. "I would never hurt her."

"You sure about that?"

I blew out a stream of white smoke. "Walsh saw us together. He might try to get to me through her."

"Which is why I already put Sad Pete and Timmy on watch at her place."

Damn, Matty was efficient. "Thank you."

"Just as long as we're clear on how this ends. I know you never apologize, but—"

"I have no intention of apologizing." Apologies were for weaker men. I was the leader. I had to make decisions and stand by them.

"She's not yours to keep."

"I know," I barked. "Leave it, yeah?"

We rode south in silence. I closed my eyes and continued to smoke. Was Belle following my instructions right now? Was she strumming those delicate fingers over her clit? Fuck, I'd give anything to see her pleasure herself. To hear her gasps and sighs as she climaxed.

God knew I didn't deserve her, but New York wasn't about what you deserved. It was about what you could *take*.

I'd risen from nothing to sit atop an empire of violence and corruption. Never had any kind of formal education. All my knowledge came from the streets and from whatever books I could find. I wouldn't live long, not with enemies around every corner, but I had no regrets.

So if Isabelle Kelly wanted my help, then I would help. For a price.

Minutes later the carriage rolled to a stop and I threw open the door. Years ago I gave Lisette, a former lover, the cash to start this bordello and she'd done well for herself. The girls were here willingly, well taken care of, and everyone shared in the profits. They wouldn't mind having an extended guest as a favor to me.

Charlie and Lisette were waiting in the entry when I went inside, Matty on my heels. Lisette came over first. "Bonsoir, mon ami," she said in her fake French accent. "I see you sent over a gift?"

I kissed her cheek. "Yeah. I need you to look after my guest for a little while."

"Bien sûr, monsieur. We have given him the Versailles room."

"You're too good to me. I appreciate it."

"Anything for you, Baxter." Drawing closer, Lisette brushed a lock of hair off my forehead. Her voice lost its French accent as she spoke quietly. "You look tired. Are you going to stay a while? I could find you some company."

It wasn't an unusual request, and the answer would've been different last night. Before Belle arrived at the fights with a pistol. "Thanks, Lizzy, but I've got more to do and it's already late. Take good care of my guest, though. Whatever he wants, yeah? I'll cover the cost."

She nodded. "Will you tell me who he is?"

"No, and it's gotta stay quiet. Make sure the girls know."

"Of course. They won't talk."

"Good. Do me a favor? Bring me a pencil and paper up there. I need him to write something down for me."

"His last will and testament?"

I chuckled. "Not quite, but close."

She trailed her fingers over my jaw. "You sure you won't stay? I have some time."

I shook my head and kissed her temple. "Can't, not even for you. If there's a problem, let me know right away."

"I will," she said with a sigh and drifted toward her office.

I approached Charlie. "Any problems?"

"He got a little rough, but the boys handled it. No idea why anyone would fight an extended stay at Lisette's."

"He won't resist for long. A flea on a dog has more restraint. I give it a week before he's fucked his way through the house."

Charlie chuckled and held out the room key. "You going up now?"

"Yeah. Thought I'd welcome him to his new temporary home."

"Want me to come with you?"

I took the key and clapped his shoulder. "Not necessary. Go home and get some sleep."

"Thanks, Bax." Starting for the door, he nodded at Matty as he walked past. "Night, Matilda."

Her expression didn't change. "Fuck off, Charlie."

I took the stairs to the second floor, Matty close behind. I didn't bother knocking. Instead, I threw open the door and strode inside. My prisoner was stretched out on the bed, his hair and clothing disheveled. He sat up slowly when I entered.

"Hello, Kelly."

CHAPTER 6

Baxter

*H*onest Dan Kelly glared back at me. "I trust you've seen the error of your flagitious ways and are ready to release me."

I stared down at my prisoner. Kelly was a blowhard. A corrupt liar, just like the rest of the politicians. I generally left them alone unless I needed something in particular. So when Kelly finished his term as comptroller, I thought I'd heard the last of him.

Then he announced he was running for mayor a month ago.

That was too far. The man who once called me vermin would not ascend to the highest seat in City Hall. No fucking way would I allow it. I ran this city, not the mayor. And certainly not Dan Kelly.

So I'd taken matters into my own hands.

I folded my arms over my chest. "Are you complaining about your upgrade in accommodations? Because I'm happy to take you back to the warehouse."

Instead of answering, he asked, "Why am I here?"

"Perhaps I'm feeling benevolent."

"Men like you don't have a benevolent bone in your body."

"You better hope I do, if you want to continue breathing." I stepped closer and put a great deal of menace in my expression. "And you should be fucking grateful. When the city learns what you've done, you're finished here."

"I don't appreciate blackmail, Baxter."

"Get used to it. Until I get what I want, I own you."

"And what is it you want?"

Looking down my nose at him, I answered, "I want you ruined. Destroyed. Humiliated."

"Then why hold me here? Why haven't you played your cards yet, Baxter?"

Did he think I was bluffing? "Anxious to lose everything so soon?"

"I'm skeptical you possess any proof whatsoever. I think you are stalling while having someone fabricate the evidence."

"I have what I need, Kelly. Though I suspect those boxes of paper we found in your home office will give me more." I went to the mirror and smoothed my hair. I was tired, but that orgasm had given me a burst of vigor. "Don't worry. Just as soon as the boys finish sorting it all, I'll call a few reporters and tell them everything I know."

"Let me go." His voice was an entitled snarl, a man unaccustomed to ceding his power to another.

But I was a man used to *taking* power. I would grasp and claw for whatever I could gain in this city—and I would not lose my leverage when I was so close. "Rescind your candidacy for mayor and I will."

"Absolutely not. I'm the front-runner."

A knock sounded and I went for the door. "Then I suggest you get comfortable and enjoy Lisette's hospitality."

"You'd like that, I suppose."

"Sit and stare at the wall, if you want. Though you should know Lisette's girls are the best in the city. No one would judge you for having some fun."

I jerked open the door and Lisette was there. She handed me a pencil and paper. "Here, mon chou."

"Thanks." I tossed the items onto Kelly's bed. "Write a letter to your daughter. Tell her you're alive."

Kelly's gaze grew suspicious. "Why?"

So she doesn't worry herself into an early grave over you, you bastard.

"I'll see that it's delivered to her."

"Again, why?"

I wanted to punch him in the face. He hadn't given one thought to Belle's well being since his kidnapping. I forced myself to shrug. "If you don't care about her, then I'll go see her myself. Put her mind at ease."

He frowned, clearly not liking the prospect of his precious daughter with me. Good. He would really hate knowing she showed me her undergarments, then sucked my finger as I tugged my cock.

Too bad I couldn't rub it in his face. But I wouldn't do that Belle. Never mind why. For now, everything we did was our little secret.

He dashed off some words on the paper. I read it to make sure he hadn't given her any incriminating information about me. He hadn't.

Instead, the letter was dry, like a list for the market. All it said was that she should stay home and not worry about him.

I shook my head and put the letter in my pocket. "Touching," I drawled. "Enjoy your stay."

Kelly didn't respond as I left. Matty closed the door and I turned the key, locking Kelly in. We left the key with Lisette and headed back out to my waiting carriage.

I climbed inside and closed my eyes, more exhausted than I thought. But the idea of my empty bed sounded as appealing as a trip to Police Headquarters. Maybe I should've stayed with Lizzy . . . .

No, I didn't want another woman. I wanted to curl up next to Belle and breathe in her sweet scent all night.

Whatever I want, whenever I want it.

"Where to?" Matty asked when I didn't speak.

Before I could think better of it, I made the decision swiftly. "Take me to the widow's house."

* * *

Isabelle

I WOKE SLOWLY, the bed warmer than usual.

I'd never felt more comfortable, more secure. I was wrapped tightly, like a butterfly in a cocoon.

My dreams . . . . Goodness, I would never repeat them to a single soul. A familiar gangster featured prominently in all of them, his eyes devouring me as I showed him more of my special undergarments. I didn't ever want to wake up.

"Easy, Belle," a man's voice whispered. "Go back to sleep."

I was instantly alert. Bax was in my bed. Wrapped around me. And I was naked. Oh my goodness, had we . . .?

No, I wasn't sore and Bax was on top of the covers. Thank heavens.

Wait, how did he get in? I needed him to leave before my maid arrived.

"What are you doing here?" I hissed.

"Sleeping. And I'd prefer to continue, if you don't mind."

"I do mind!" I tried to shove him off. "This was not part of our deal."

He put his face in my hair and growled in his throat. It tugged something deep in my core. I sucked in a breath, and instantly became aware of my bare skin rubbing against the soft bedclothes, sensation everywhere.

Now I remembered. I'd followed Bax's orders last night, slipping into bed naked and pleasuring myself before falling asleep. Subsequently, my dreams had been filled with the dark-eyed gangster.

It was as if I'd summoned him from the underworld, the devil.

While confusion, outrage and desire battled inside me, Bax's hands slid atop the coverlet to rest on my hip. Goose bumps trailed in his wake, and he threw one of his big legs over both of mine, trapping me. "Are you naked under there?"

I didn't want to answer. I couldn't. It was far too embarrassing.

"You can tell me, sweetheart," he purred, the words silky and smooth, like satin over bare skin. "The possibility has been driving me out of my skull all night."

He'd been here all night?

Bare shoulders filled my vision as he loomed over me. Oh, my. Bax had shed his clothing before getting in my bed. Had he shed *all* of his clothing? I tried to raise up and look. All I saw was golden skin stretched over glorious muscle.

"I kept my trousers on," he murmured into the sensitive skin of my throat. "I didn't wish to frighten your delicate sensibilities."

I shivered at the scrape of his morning whiskers, so delicious and unexpected. For some reason, I didn't want him to think of me as a boring, sheltered innocent. Even though the description was mostly true.

"My sensibilities aren't so delicate, as I proved last night."

"You're so goddamn pretty with your hair down." His lips brushed the underside of my jaw. "You should never pin it up."

Closing my eyes, I sank into the mattress. My body vibrated with the need to touch him, to satisfy my curiosity about his lean frame. Did he feel as hard and rough as he looked?

He kissed along my collarbone. "Mmm, this is my new favorite way to wake up."

I had to admit, it wasn't terrible. Wildly inappropriate, but not terrible.

A knock sounded on my door. I froze, cold terror sliding through my veins. Bax continued to kiss my skin, clearly unconcerned.

"Miss, are you awake?" It was my maid, Mary.

"Give me a few minutes, please!" I called back.

"Very good, miss." I heard the breakfast tray rattling as my maid departed down the hall.

I shoved Bax's shoulder. "Get out of here. You had no right to come into my bedroom."

He rolled onto his back and stretched, showing off his long half-naked body. "I said anything I want, yeah?"

"That does not include sleeping."

"It does if I say so."

"You cannot sleep in my bed. It is unseemly and improper."

The side of his mouth lifted ever so slightly. "I love the prim and proper way you talk. But you aren't a good girl, are you, Belle?"

"You hardly know anything about me."

He chuckled. "Sweetheat, you wear undergarments that would make a Tenderloin floozy blush. You sneak out with your father's pistol and shove it in my face at the fights. Best of all, you fingered your clitoris last night because a gangster asked you to."

Humiliation scalded my skin. I didn't like that he saw me so clearly. "You need to leave."

He moved a hand to his chest and slowly dragged it toward his belly. "Are you sure? I might be persuaded to stay." The sight of his long fingers brushing over his big body sent ripples of excitement along my spine to war with my anger. I could still picture his big hand wrapped around his male appendage, stroking.

"Get out, Bax." Was my voice unsteady? Why was my heart beating so fast?

Rolling toward me, his eyelids swept open. We stared at one another, the air crackling with danger and possibility, but I couldn't predict what he was planning to do. Still, I didn't waver. He could not walk all over me, no matter our agreement.

Fighting my nerves, I put as much bravado as possible in my expression. Slowly, he unfolded and raised off the bed. He found his shirt on the floor, tugged it over his head and shoved it into his trousers. Then he pulled up his suspenders and sat on the bed to put on his shoes.

Once he was dressed, he started around toward my side of the bed. His hair tousled from sleep, he was more attractive than any man had a right to be at this time of morning. I clutched the bedclothes like a shield, more terrified of the excitement rioting inside me than of Bax.

He neared and I held my breath. What was he going to do? My bare toes curled into the bedclothes, my mind racing through possibilities. He placed his hand above my head. There was a strange light in his eyes, and it caused the place between my legs to grow damp.

He leaned down, his voice quiet. "You need to come to terms with our agreement. That is, if you still wish to find your father."

"I do."

"I'm glad to hear it." He bent and dragged his nose over my cheek. "Sundown. Be ready. I'm coming for you."

The contact sent little shocks of pleasure over my skin, and I marveled at how such a simple touch could turn me inside out. There was hidden meaning in his words, but I couldn't decipher it at the moment, not with him so near, making my pulse race.

He needed to leave before I did something rash. Like kissing him.

Without another word, he pushed off the bed. "By the way, there's a letter for you on the nightstand. Have a good day, widow."

He walked out. I sagged, the air leaving my lungs in a rush. Mercy, that man. He had some nerve. We would have a serious discussion later regarding his sleeping arrangements. He was not allowed to visit my bedchamber whenever he wished.

My gaze drifted toward the bed. His side was rumpled, exactly like mine. Pillow indented, exactly like mine. We'd cuddled, for heaven's sake.

And if I were being honest? I liked it.

A folded piece of paper rested on the nightstand. What was this? I crawled over and quickly opened it. It was my father's handwriting!

Isabelle,

Do not worry about me. Stay at home, where you're safe.

D. Kelly

I chewed my lip. Papa wasn't much of a letter writer, so the terse brevity shouldn't have bothered me.

Yet it did.

Perhaps he was too injured to write? Or maybe he knew the kidnappers would read the letter and didn't wish to be too mushy?

Whatever the reason, I should be grateful to hear from him. My father was alive, which was what mattered. Not my silly feelings.

How had Bax managed to get this letter? Had he learned the identity of the kidnappers?

I would force him to tell me everything tonight.

Just the thought of seeing him again had my stomach dancing with anticipation. What undergarments should I wear?

A knock sounded, startling me. Mary, no doubt, had returned with breakfast.

I lunged for my wrapper, covered myself, then tried to relax on my pillows. "Come in."

Mary entered and held up the tray. "Would you like your breakfast in bed? Or shall I set it on the table?"

I glanced at the bed as if it were the scene of a heinous crime. Bax's scent was undoubtedly all over the bedclothes. I was caught between wanting to never leave the bed and running far away from it.

I said, "The table, please. Thank you, Mary."

"Very good, miss."

When I sat at the table, I noticed a sealed note by my tea cup. "What's this?"

"Arrived for you this morning. Do you require anything else at the moment?"

I was already unfolding the heavy paper. "No, that's all. I'll ring when I'm ready to get dressed."

Mary closed the door softly and I smoothed out the note in my hands. Was this another letter from my father?

We have information about your father. 550 West 37ᵗʰ Street at 3:00 p.m. today. Come alone.

This was not from Papa. Nor was it from Bax. No, this had to be from the kidnapper. Or someone who knew the kidnapper.

Hope fluttered in my chest like tiny butterflies. Could I find my father on my own?

Finding Papa meant putting an end to all of this. No Bax, no ruined reputation. My life could return to normal. Daniel Kelly would save the city again, and I would go back to rambling about in this big house by myself. We would occasionally see one another. Perhaps he might even be grateful and praise my bravery and intelligence.

Still, I wasn't a fool. This was dangerous. I had no idea who wrote the note. It could be from someone with information . . . or it could be someone looking to hurt me.

I had to try. Relying on Bax to help me was problematic for many reasons. My eyes drifted to the bed, still rumpled from where he slept.

"I'm so hard for you, Belle."

Watching him perform the act of self-pleasure had aroused me, far more than I ever dreamed. But I couldn't let this go further.

Resisting him was growing more and more difficult. I had no protection against his particular brand of danger, one that came with slick smiles and racing heartbeats. One that had me contemplating my own ruin.

"Anything I want, whenever I want it."

I needed to get that man out of my life.

Indeed, decision made. I'd take my gun and go to that address on Thirty-Seventh Street today. And I'd leave a note here at the house in case I didn't return. If disaster struck, the police could use it to look for me.

And if all went to plan, then I would never see Billy Baxter again.

CHAPTER 7

Isabelle

The building looked deserted.

I tried to remain calm. The pistol sat heavy in my coat pocket, my nerves stretched tight as I approached the door. Whoever wrote the note wasn't expecting me for another forty-five minutes. Arriving early would give me the element of surprise.

My mouth was dry, but I forced my feet to move forward. I slipped through the unlocked front door and entered what turned out to be an empty room. As quietly as possible I started across the worn wooden floor. I retrieved the pistol from my pocket and held it in front of me. Was someone here?

Dust tickled my nose, the musty air uncomfortable in my lungs. The place clearly hadn't been used in some time. I went up a set of stairs in the back, my shoes nearly silent on the treads.

A door stood open at the top. No one was in there, just a desk, a few chairs and cabinets. Excellent. I could hide under that desk.

Moving into the room, I heard a squeak behind me. I started to spin, but I wasn't fast enough. Thick arms grabbed me from behind and pinned my hands to my sides. My pistol clattered uselessly to the floor. *Dash it!* I couldn't pull free, so I began to struggle.

"Caught you," a deep voice said before strong fingers wrapped around my throat, squeezing.

I tried to suck in air but couldn't. Chest burning, I began to panic. Was this stranger intending to kill me? I couldn't die, not without finding my father first.

Not without seeing Bax again.

"I wonder how much he'll pay to get you back," the man sneered and started dragging me across the floor. "No guarantee on what condition you'll be in by that time, of course. We're all eager for a turn."

Oh, God. Icy terror slid down my spine. I had to get to my gun.

I went boneless. His grip slipped and I fell to the floor at his feet. I didn't waste a second. As quickly as I could, I scrambled for my pistol. My fingers clenched on the cool metal, but he pounced on me, an angry snarl filling the air. His fist tightened in my hair, pulling hard until tears sprang to my eyes. I screamed as loudly as I could manage.

"You bitch!" The side of my head slammed into the floor. Pain exploded in my skull and I grew dizzy. No, no, no! I had to keep fighting.

He was on top of me, his heavy bulk preventing me from drawing in a full breath. I gripped the gun, but couldn't maneuver my arm to shoot him. He lifted my head again, probably to slam it onto the floor once more, so I acted on pure instinct.

I tilted my hand and aimed toward us both, then pulled the trigger.

His body jerked, then he slammed my head onto the ground once more.

The edges of the room dimmed. Distantly, I heard a shout. Was someone downstairs? Thankfully, my attacker let me go and rolled off. I immediately sucked in air to fill my lungs as the room wavered. Feet pounded on the wooden floor.

Then the blackness rose to swallow me.

* * *

Baxter

"WHERE THE FUCK IS SHE?" I charged into the building, my chest tight with fury and panic.

"Upstairs," Sad Pete replied, pointing me toward the back. "I'm sorry, Bax. It all happened so fast. One minute she went inside, the next a gun was going off."

I took the stairs three at a time. "And you didn't think to get in here and put a stop to it?"

"Wasn't time, I swear! When we stopped, I followed her while Timmy went to fetch you."

"She never should've been allowed inside here. I thought you were watching her house!"

"We were. She gave us the slip and caught a hack. We caught up as soon as we could."

"I will deal with you later," I snarled and pushed into the room upstairs.

Christ almighty. There she was, my Belle. Crumpled and hurt on the floor.

Fuck, fuck, fuck.

I was at her side in a flash, checking for blood and injuries. Her eyes were closed, her limbs lax. There were bruises forming on the sensitive skin of her throat. A wicked knot was forming on the side of her head. But she was breathing.

She was alive.

"Blood on the floor belongs to whoever had her," Timmy said. "I think she shot him."

Under the heavy fabric of her skirts, I located her pistol. *Good girl.*

"She fought him, that's for sure," Matty murmured behind me. I wasn't surprised she was here. No doubt she followed the second I went running from the saloon.

"Where is the bastard who did this to her?" I glared at Sad Pete as I hoisted Belle up in my arms.

He paled. "Lost him in the alley two streets over."

I wanted to strangle both of my men for this, but I didn't have the time. "Both of you out of my sight. Go and find him. No doubt he works for Walsh. Bring him to me alive. Matty, with me."

I carried Belle down the stairs and out of the building. Matty's carriage was at the curb, so I climbed up and settled, still cradling Belle in my lap. Matty followed, yelling, "As fast as you can!" to Robbie up in the box.

When we started moving she said, "You know how I feel about you leaving the saloon unguarded."

I frowned. This was not the time for one of her lectures regarding my safety. Not when Belle had almost been killed. "There wasn't a choice."

"You plan to keep her with you, I assume?"

"Yes, until further notice."

"She won't like it. She—"

"She will stay until I say otherwise."

"You could let her father go."

I glared at my longtime friend. "No."

Matty pursed her lips. "Whoever hurt her was trying to hurt *you*. This isn't about her father. And keeping Kelly hostage will only make things worse."

Logically, I knew this. But I wasn't capable of thinking straight when it came to Belle. "She's safest in my care."

"Billy," Matty said on a disapproving sigh.

"Not another word, Matilda." I didn't want to hear it. I was in charge, and they'd all pledged their loyalty to me. That meant not questioning my every goddamn decision.

Belle began to stir when we pulled up to the saloon. The Devil's Hand was my domain in Hell's Kitchen. The saloon and back rooms offered a safe meeting place, while the second floor was my office and some living quarters. The third floor was where I stayed. No one was ever allowed up there, except for Matty. And now Belle.

"Bax?" Belle's fingers curled into my vest as she stirred.

I continued up the stairs, ignoring the looks from my men. "It's me, widow. Just relax."

Matty followed, and I was grateful for the help in getting my door unlocked. Before she left, Matty said, "I'll go see what I can find out."

"Good. Send the doc up." I had one nearby for emergencies. "Also deal with Timmy and Sad Pete."

Matty nodded and disappeared, leaving me alone with Belle. Striding into my bedroom, I placed her on my bed. Her eyelids fluttered open, finally showing me her gorgeous eyes, and it was such a goddamn relief that my knees went weak. I sat heavily on the mattress.

She licked her lips. "Where are we?" Her voice was rough, like pebbles were stuck in her throat. It had to hurt like a son of a bitch to speak.

Guilt pricked at the nape of my neck. Belle had been hurt because of me. I got up and poured her a glass of water from the stand. "Don't talk. Rest your throat."

"Then . . . answer."

Returning with a full glass, I helped her sit upright enough to drink. "You're in my apartment, atop my saloon."

She finished half the water, then relaxed. "Home."

Walsh—or any of my other enemies—could find her there. It was too much of a risk. "It's not safe."

She turned her head to the side and closed her eyes. A single tear slipped from the corner onto my pillow. I wiped the wetness from her skin with a fingertip. Then I bent to press my lips to her temple. "Someone tried to hurt you. Until I find out who, I'm not letting you out of my sight."

"Why . . . you care?"

I wasn't sure.

I just knew I couldn't let anyone hurt her. Ever.

"Until we find your father, you're mine," I whispered into her skin, a promise sworn into flesh and bone. "And I will burn down this entire city to keep you safe."

She turned her head and kissed me.

I nearly fell off the bed. Jesus, I hadn't expected this. But her lips were on mine, our noses rubbing, and I kissed her back. Her mouth was soft and sweet, and I soaked in the reassurance that she was still here. Still alive.

Before it turned into something more, I eased away. "I'll let you sleep, sweetheart."

"No, stay." Her fingers clutched my arm. "I don't want to be alone."

I understood. She'd almost died. It could rattle a person.

Standing, I removed my coat and boots. Then I went to the other side of the bed and stretched out next to her. She rolled toward me and curled into my side, as sweet and trusting as a kitten. I didn't know a damn thing about heaven, but I had to imagine it was this right here. Belle in my bed, in my arms.

My cock was growing stiff, but I ignored it. "Try to sleep."

"Talk to me. Tell me . . . a story."

"I'm no good at talking." Ask me to win a fight or fire a pistol, cheat the coppers or rob a bank. But spin a yarn full of fantasy?

My life was about hard truths and cold realities. About staying alive long enough to see another day. Fairy tales were for the privileged.

"Please, Bax?" she asked through a yawn.

Christ. How could I refuse such a sweet request?

I decided to go with the partial truth. My voice low, I said, "There once was a powerful man, one the entire city feared. His every waking moment was consumed by thoughts of money and power."

She remained quiet, her soft exhales warming my skin.

I stroked her back with my palm. "This man had been raised with nothing, a forgotten soul in a city of forgotten souls. Vermin, they called him. As a boy he vowed to conquer the island, to make every single person bow and scrape at his feet. To get revenge on those who wronged him. And he succeeded. He'd never let anyone hurt him or make him vulnerable again."

Belle's breath was even and steady, so I peeked at her face. Her eyes were closed, lips parted slightly. She'd fallen asleep.

"Then he met a woman. A fierce angel who was so much more than she seemed. And his world turned upside down."

A sense of contentment washed over me, a sense of rightness. I always trusted my gut, and it told me this was exactly where I was supposed to be. With this woman, here in my saloon.

I stared at the ceiling, feeling no desire to move whatsoever. "What the hell are you doing to me, widow?"

CHAPTER 8

Isabelle

I came awake slowly, every bit of me sore. Especially my head. In a flash it came rushing back—the building, the attack, firing the pistol—and panic bubbled up to rob me of air.

"Calm down," a feminine voice said. "You're safe. You're at Bax's place."

Oh, thank goodness. I was *alive*. I hadn't died on the dirty floor of that empty building.

Wait, I was at Bax's place? As in, Bax's *bed*? I vaguely remembered him lying here with me, talking to me as I tried to rest. It seemed like a far-off dream, one I knew I needed to recall but couldn't.

Matty, Bax's guard, was sitting in a chair beside the bed. I blinked at her. "Why?"

"Why did he bring you here, or why does your skull hurt like hell?"

I struggled to sit up, then reached for the water glass by the bed. Matty merely watched, her flat, emotionless stare making me slightly nervous.

After I drank, I set the glass back down with a shaky hand. "Why am I here?"

"Haven't you figured it out yet?"

"No."

Matty folded her hands and leaned back in the chair. "Why were you in that building?"

"A note was delivered, saying they had information regarding my father's whereabouts."

"And the man who attacked you? Did he say anything?"

I searched my memories. Snippets of those terrifying moments came back to me like flashes. Being grabbed, the smothering feeling of going without air for so long. His deep voice. *Caught you.* I took a deep breath and fought the wave of dizziness that came over me. "He said 'I wonder how much he'll pay to get you back.'"

"Any idea who 'he' is?"

"No."

"Anything else?"

"Not that I can recall."

Matty slapped her palms on her thighs and pushed to her feet. "I'll let Bax know you're awake. He's been a fucking bear downstairs."

"How long have I been sleeping?"

"About twenty-two hours."

Almost an entire day! Goodness. How was that possible?

Matty looked me up and down. "You need help getting to the toilet?" The expression she wore made it clear that assisting me was the last thing she wanted to do.

"No, I can manage. Thank you."

She started toward the door, her boots thudding on the carpets. Then she paused. "I've been looking after Baxter for a long time. Don't hurt him, Miss Kelly. If you do, you'll have to answer to me—and I won't go easy on you."

Without waiting on a response, Matty disappeared into the other room. The outer door opened and closed, and I blew out a long breath of relief. Matty was intimidating and slightly terrifying.

Shoving off the bedclothes, I pushed to my feet. Once my knees were steady, I slowly made my way toward the washroom, which I found behind one of the closed doors in the outer room.

There was a rain bath inside, too, so I decided to soak my sore muscles under the hot spray. It was heavenly.

When I finished, I wrapped myself in Bax's silk dressing gown and emerged from the washroom. A figure was propped against the wall, frowning at me.

Bax stepped forward and scooped me up in one smooth motion. I wrapped my arms around his neck, not ashamed to admit that I liked his display of strength.

"You should've called for help." He strode toward the bedroom. "Don't get on your feet again until I know you won't collapse, yeah?"

I didn't hate his concern, even though it was misplaced. "I'm fine, Bax."

"I'll decide when you're well enough, widow."

I pushed my face into the warmth of his throat, not wanting him to see my pleased grin. There was so much upheaval and chaos in my life, but he was here, solid and sure. He was like the bedrock under Manhattan or the steel used to construct the Brooklyn Bridge. I knew we'd just met, but I felt cared for, protected. Like I mattered to him.

"You aren't a good girl, are you, Belle?"

His earlier words flitted through my mind. He was right. I wasn't proper and I was tired of pretending otherwise. I almost *died* yesterday. And what did I have to show for my life? Some fancy undergarments that no one ever saw?

Instead, I was waiting around in my big home. Waiting for Papa to notice me and treat me like I was more important than his causes. Waiting for a suitor to take me on boring drives in the park and tedious walks along the avenue. Waiting, waiting, waiting . . . .

But I had the chance to live at this very moment with the most exciting man I'd ever met. Yes, it was temporary, but shouldn't I grasp every opportunity when it came?

I didn't want to fight this any longer. I wanted *more.* More naughty undergarments, more cuddling. More of Bax's attention and filthy words. Until we found my father, perhaps I could view this as an adventure.

I wanted, even for a short time, to belong to Billy Baxter.

He bent and placed me on the mattress, but I wasn't ready to let go. I held onto his neck. "Don't go." The word fell easily from my mouth. "Stay with me."

He unwound my arms from his neck, his face stern as he put distance between himself and the bed. "I'll sit in the chair."

"No, please. Lay here with me on the mattress."

He stared down at me, his gaze piercing my soul. "Why?"

"It's after sundown."

"And?"

Was he truly going to make me say it? "You said you were coming for me."

Something dark flashed in his gaze, like he found the reminder arousing, and my toes curled. Still, he didn't budge. "You're hurt. You should rest."

"I feel excellent. I slept for almost a day and stood in a hot rain bath. Please?" I could sense his indecision, so I pressed. "I need you."

"Yeah? You want me to hold you?"

"And other things." I must've been the color of a tomato, if the heat I felt under my skin was any indication.

"Yeah? What other things?"

"Kissing me, touching me."

"I see." Dropping on the mattress next to me, he leaned in to lick the lobe of my ear. "Is your pussy wet?"

Goodness, the manner in which this man talked. I nodded.

"*Fuck*." He began kissing my jaw, my throat. "I can help with that."

Sparks ignited deep inside me, every part of my body hyper aware of this complicated man. Everything about him appealed to me, from the way he smelled—like tobacco and leather—to the shape of his muscles under his clothing. The long sweep of his lashes and the rough rasp of his voice. A knot of craving formed between my legs, an ache that was bone deep.

"I like the way you look in my dressing gown," he murmured

against my throat. His hand slid over my hip and along my ribs, and I shuddered.

He pulled on the ties and the sides fell apart, revealing my bare skin. I started to cover myself out of habit, but he held my hands. "There's no reason to hide. You're the most beautiful thing I've ever seen."

"You can't truly mean that."

He rocked his erection into my hip. "I mean it, sweetheart. Feel that?"

"Oh." I couldn't contain a small smile, which he noticed, of course.

"You like that I'm always hard around you? That my cock and balls ache all the time?"

"Yes."

He leaned over, chuckling softly. "There's my naughty girl."

Then he kissed me, but this was nothing like our earlier kiss. This was deep and thorough, aggressive. I could taste his hunger and possession, the fierce need, and I fed it right back to him in equal measure.

Pleasure raced through me as my heart pounded in my ears, and I held on as his tongue slipped past my lips to find mine. It was so intimate, almost shocking, but I loved the way he surrounded me, his tongue flicking and swirling. Heat jumped between us in a perfect circuit and I arched closer, needing more.

He broke off and trailed his lips along my jaw, then down my throat. Goose bumps followed in his wake and I panted for air. My back bowed as he kissed the tops of my breasts, a delicious torture that wasn't quite enough. "Bax," I whined.

His mouth met my nipple and drew me inside, sucking. The answering tug in my core caused me to gasp, and desire pooled between my thighs. He didn't let up and I squirmed beneath him, desperate. By the time he moved to the other nipple, I was mindlessly begging. "Oh, please."

Leaving my breast, he descended the length of my body until his shoulders were pressing my thighs wide. Instinctively I tried to close my legs.

"Relax," he breathed and pressed a kiss to my folds. "I'll take care of you."

The first swipe of his tongue sent shocks through me, like I was electrified. "What . . .?"

Bax growled and did it again. "Your pussy is soaking. Just fucking dripping." He licked my entrance, then hummed. "So damn delicious."

Was this a thing people did in the bedroom? I hadn't imagined it, never even considered it a possibility. Yet Bax proceeded as if this was perfectly normal, something we would both enjoy.

The button of nerves atop my sex seemed in perfect agreement. It was throbbing, pulsing, as if trying to work its way inside Bax's mouth.

He shifted his attention there, and my brain lit up with bright colors. I moaned as he dragged his tongue over me, painting the flesh, drawing on my body. The pleasure was intense, nothing I'd ever experienced before, and I was soon thrashing beneath him, a mindless mess. My fingers curled into the bedclothes as every muscle strained toward the peak.

His lips and tongue kept at it, and then I felt him probing my entrance. A finger slipped inside and the resulting fullness came as both a surprise and a relief. I hadn't realized how empty I was there until he entered me, and now I never wanted him to leave. "Oh, God," I said on a long delirious moan, my hand drifting to the top of his head.

When he sucked on that tiny bud, my brain left my body. I became a quivering mass of nerves and sensation, climbing higher and higher, racing toward the finish as his finger worked in and out.

"You call out my name when it happens, Belle," he growled into my flesh. "No one else's."

I rocked my hips, greedy, well past all reason and propriety. I only knew I had to reach the peak or I'd die. This was so much better than anything I'd ever felt before.

The climax rushed over me with the power of a locomotive. "Bax!" I shouted, the bliss flinging me into the ether, and my body trembled uncontrollably. I clutched at him, riding out the waves, chanting his name like a prayer.

When the pleasure ebbed, he continued licking me, rubbing his nose and chin on my skin, until I twitched with sensitivity. Then he dropped onto his back beside me, his chest heaving.

I couldn't speak, not yet. My mind was a jumble of fragments, scattered thoughts just out of reach. I felt dazed and disoriented in the very best manner.

"Fuck, that was good," he said.

My sentiments exactly. There was so much that I had yet to experience in this world—and there was no time to lose. When my father returned I would go back to lonely nights and boring days.

I curled toward Bax, my fingers playing with the buttons on his vest. "How soon can you do that again?"

* * *

Baxter

THE DELICIOUS FLAVOR of her filled my head. I licked my lips and smiled. "I'd happily tongue you day and night, if you allowed it."

"Why on earth would anyone ever prevent you?"

Goddamn, this woman. I needed a minute to calm down. My cock was impossibly hard, my balls aching and heavy. Closing my eyes, I took a few deep breaths and resisted the urge to hump the mattress like an animal.

I felt her shift closer, the scent of her pussy filling the air like the sweetest perfume. I wanted to bathe in it.

Her hand swept over my chest and ribs. "Are you unwell?"

"I'm fine. Merely need to—"

Her palm brushed over the ridge of my cock through my trousers. I nearly jumped off the bed, hissing through my teeth.

She snatched her hand away. "I'm sorry. I thought since you had touched me . . . ." She bit her lip.

I hated the hurt and confusion in her gaze. Placing my hand on her jaw, I moved in close. "I want your hand on my cock—you have no idea how much—but there's no reason to rush. We have plenty of time."

"I feel as though I've been waiting forever," she whispered. "And do you know what I thought about when I almost died in that abandoned building?"

Every muscle in my body clenched, my anger returning full force. I didn't want to think about her in that place, hurt and almost dying. We needed to have a serious conversation about the irresponsibility of going there in the first place, but now was not the time.

I forced myself to relax. "What did you think about, gorgeous?"

"You."

She tried to duck her head, but I wouldn't let her. Not after saying something like that. I held tight so I could see her expression. "What about me?"

"I didn't want to die without seeing you again. I don't want to waste more time before doing this." Her eyes were unclouded, bright with reason and awareness. Lust and determination.

"This, meaning letting me lick your pussy."

"Yes—and letting me do things to you in exchange." She leaned in to press her lips to my jaw, and sparks raced down my legs. "May I touch you?"

Shit. Was I truly contemplating this? Every thump of my heart echoed along my erection, but I didn't want her to regret anything that happened.

"You've had a scare," I said. "And you're hurt. Let's wait until you start thinking clearly again."

"I am thinking clearly. I'm tired of not living my life." She dragged her fingertips over my thigh, trailing higher toward my groin.

My willpower crumbled. If she wanted it, she could have it. Chest heaving, I rolled to my back and ripped open the fastenings to my trousers. I freed my cock as quickly as I could manage. Cool air washed over my skin as I stroked myself.

Then I released my shaft and waited. She would need to do the rest, provided she really wanted to. "There you go."

She nibbled the inside of her cheek and stared at my cock, almost as if deciding on how best to proceed. "I should just do what you did in the carriage?"

"Yeah. Show it who's boss, sweetheart."

I held my breath and waited. I craved the feel of her hands and mouth, needed it like air. So what would she do?

"It's so pretty," she whispered, scooting closer to my belly. "I hadn't expected that."

Fuuuck. My little virgin widow. I longed to shove inside her pussy and claim her. Thrust into her until she screamed. Teach her how good it was going to be between us.

Her brows shot up. "It just moved! Why did it move?"

Because it was thinking of splitting you in two, filling you up with come.

"It does that sometimes," I said, my voice threaded with lust.

Her look of eager fascination had me gritting my back teeth. One delicate fingertip reached to stroke along the shaft, the touch light and brief. "It moved again," she said.

I groaned and wrapped a fist around the base, unable to stand it any longer. I needed friction. "Belle."

"No, let me." She shoved my hand away. "Please. I want to, Bax."

Then she dragged her fingers around me lightly, like she was petting my dick. My thigh muscles clenched in frustration. "Harder. Grip me around the base and pull like you're angry at it."

"Oh. Won't that hurt?"

I nearly laughed as I stretched my arms over my head. "Sweetheart, I've been shot, stabbed and hit over the head with a brickbat. You can't hurt me. Now, lick your palm and make me come."

Never breaking my stare, she brought her hand to her mouth. When her pink tongue emerged to slowly wet her skin, I thought I might spend right then. It was the most erotic thing I'd ever seen in my life. "Yeah, that's it," I whispered. "Get it nice and slick."

She licked once more, then reached for my cock. She worked me good this time, her grip tight and rough, just as I preferred. Between the glide of her spit-coated skin and the determined glint in her eyes, I figured it wouldn't take long. I could already feel my balls tightening in readiness. "Goddamn, the things I want to do to you."

"Like?" Her hand kept pumping, her wrist twisting over my crown. Just as I'd done in the carriage.

It was so good. So perfect. Sweet little naughty widow. My brain couldn't function, every nerve and cell focused on the movement of her hand. Words started tumbling from my mouth. "I want to feed my cock between your legs, but I'd go slow, yeah? I'd rub the head all through your pussy, get your cream all over it, have you panting and begging. Then I'd push inside your cunt—but not too fast. I want you to feel every bit of it, stretch you wide, while I suck on your nipples. I want to give you so much pleasure, Belle. So much that you pass out on me."

She shifted on her knees but kept stroking with her hand. So I didn't understand what was happening until it was too late.

Suddenly she was straddling my hips, her pussy hovering close to my cock. Lust shot through my groin as I fought the urge to thrust up and claim her. "*Belle.*"

Her voice dropped to a husky whisper. "Problem, William?"

God, I loved when she called me by my given name. No one but her had ever used it. "Not if you're ready to fuck."

I thought it would scare her, but it had the opposite effect. Her eyes went hooded as her tongue darted out to lick her lips. "I'm prepared for such an event to transpire."

"Yeah?" I didn't believe her, but I was fixated on the sight of her bare glistening folds hovering above my shaft. So close . . . .

Suddenly, she shrugged out of my silk dressing gown, letting it fall behind her. Naked. She was *naked.*

Jesus fuck.

I studied her face, waiting for the trick. Was this a dream? Isabelle Kelly, naked in my bed? It was too good to be true.

But this was real—and it was too soon. I knew in my bones that she would regret it later on. Better to wait and seduce her properly.

Most of all, I didn't want to do this before she knew about her father.

Billy Baxter, owner of a fucking conscience. Who would've guessed? Too bad the timing was utter shit.

But even I knew lying to her while sleeping with her was wrong.

Putting a hand on her hip, I said, "Belle, stop. Wait a minute."

She reached for the buttons on my vest. "You're right. You're still wearing clothes."

"No, wait. You aren't ready." *And I kidnapped your father.*

"You don't want me?"

The doubt in her voice nearly destroyed me. I cupped her jaw with one palm and rubbed the soft skin with my fingers. "You, Isabelle Kelly, are all I've ever wanted. But you're too good for a man like me. Your first time should be soft and sweet, with a husband who plans to—"

Before I could prevent it, she lowered her pussy onto the underside of my bare shaft, grinding down with her wet heat, and my back arched. "Shit!" I hissed, white-hot sparks punching through me. "Have mercy, widow."

Then she rocked her hips a few times, tempting me, teasing me, and the tip of my dick caught the edge of her entrance. We both froze. My nostrils flared as I dragged air into my lungs, and I prayed for a sliver of control. "Isabelle, no. There are things you don't know."

"Do you have a disease?"

My fingertips dug into the skin of her hips, where I held on like a man about to drown. "No, I mean about me. Things I've done."

"Bax," she whispered, leaning down to press a light kiss to my lips. "I know what kind of man you are, and I know how you feel about me. This feels right, here and now. With you."

"*Christ.*" I couldn't take it. In all my years, I'd never felt more on the edge. She was killing me, with her naked body atop mine, giving me all her sweetness. I was selfish. I needed this, needed her.

But I didn't want her to hate me for doing this now. It was better to wait until after the news of her father's misdeeds went public.

She must've taken my silence as agreement because she adjusted her body, widened her thighs and tilted her pelvis. My crown breached her entrance.

My muscles clenched and she moved again, bringing me in deeper. Her walls gripped my cock, sucking me in, and I lost the battle. Belle had shattered my self-control.

Except I hadn't fucked a virgin before, so we had to go slow. I closed my eyes tightly. "I don't want to hurt you."

"You're not. It feels strange, but it doesn't hurt."

I used my thumb to make tiny circles over her clitoris. I wanted to keep her nice and wet, so I could slide in easier. "Go at your pace. Let your body stretch around me."

Her lips parted on a moan and she began rocking, sinking lower, tiny movements that drove me to the edge of sanity. But I held still, letting her do this. Rumor was a virgin never found the first time pleasurable, but I was determined to disprove it. I cared about her and I'd be damned if she didn't enjoy this.

"That's it." I kept rubbing her clitoris. "My cock is yours, sweetheart. It's yours to use whenever you want it. Whenever your pussy feels empty inside."

"Oh, God. Bax." She threw her head back and braced her hands on my stomach. "I do. I do feel so empty inside."

"Then use it, good girl. Fill yourself with me until I'm all you can feel."

"I like when you call me that."

"Yeah? Then be my good girl and fuck yourself on my cock."

CHAPTER 9

Isabelle

$\mathcal{I}$t was all so strange, but I knew this was right. My heart told me it was exactly the moment, exactly the man. He'd proven it time and time again since we'd met.

"I will burn down this entire city to keep you safe."

Was it possible for me to fall in love in such a short amount of time?

He was so sweet and tender like this, quite unlike the hardened criminal he presented to the world. The angles of his face were taut with desire, but the softness in his eyes undid me, melting my insides like hot wax. He was being so careful with me, ensuring I enjoyed it.

"Oh, goodness," I breathed as he continued to brush his thumb over my clitoris. I could feel every swipe deep in my core and along my legs. Pressing down, I took more of him this time, until my body couldn't easily fit any more.

His gaze locked on where we were joined. "Have you ever put your fingers inside yourself?"

"That night you told me to imagine it was you? I slipped two fingers inside."

I wanted him naked. I began unbuttoning his vest, but he held my hands. "Belle, I'm dying to get inside you. Deep inside, like where your fingers went that night."

I frowned and looked at the size of him between my legs. "I don't understand. You are inside, at least as far as you can go."

His chuckle sounded pained. "No, sweetheart. I'm not. I'm only halfway."

"What?" The rest of him was thicker. No way would we fit. "Bax, I don't think I can take any more."

"You can." He pinched my bundle of nerves and a mixture of pleasure and pain exploded in every part of me. With his free hand, he tugged on my nipple, squeezing my breast until I moaned again. I sank lower, and he said, "See?"

He was all around me, taking up all the room inside my body. "It's too much."

"We still have more to go."

"Then you'll have to do it. I can't."

Holding my hips steady, he pressed up slowly and I tried not to whimper. I appreciated his consideration, but I just wanted it done. "Please."

He smoothed my hair off my face. "Belle, we can stop. This doesn't need to happen right now."

Yes, it did. I was tired of waiting for my life to happen, of letting others make decisions for me. Bax was allowing me to choose—and I chose this. "Now, Bax. Do it now."

"Isabelle, no. Let's go slow."

I could hear the hesitation in his voice. He wasn't going to finish it.

Taking a deep breath, I lifted up on my knees slightly then drove down as hard as possible. Pain stole through me as our hips met, a pinch between my legs that didn't let up. I hissed and held perfectly still.

"Fuck, Belle!" He arched his back, the tendons in his throat standing out in sharp relief. "I didn't want you to get hurt."

"I know." I panted and prayed the burn would subside. "But it's done now."

"You are killing me. What am I going to do with you?"

I wriggled a bit, the feeling morphing into an intense stretch now. "And you did promise to show me your favorite use of your favorite word."

He paused, his mouth curling into a grin. "So I did. How are you feeling?"

"Better. Full. Like I need to move."

"You're not in pain?"

I shifted, making certain. "No, and you don't need to be careful with me."

"Good." In a flash, he rolled us over. Keeping his erection buried inside me, he growled, "Because I need to fuck you hard."

He pressed me into the mattress, but I liked it. "Then take your clothes off and do it properly."

"No time." He eased out and gave a thrust that rattled my teeth. "When we start up again I'll get naked for you."

Then he started moving, the length of him dragging across the sensitive tissues inside me, and I was lost in a sea of sensation. My body surrendered to his, accommodating his thick shaft, welcoming him, and pleasure coiled inside me like a spring. With me naked and him fully clothed, it felt debauched. Secret and naughty.

Just like my undergarments.

The silk of his vest swiped across my swollen nipples, and he hit a spot in my channel each time that caused me to see stars. "Oh God, Bax."

"Yeah? You feeling it, widow?"

Long dark hair fell over his brow and his gaze was hooded with lust. He looked like the devil himself and I clutched at him, never wanting this to end. It was a high I had never imagined, so much better than when I touched myself.

"I feel it." I lifted slightly and pressed my lips to the skin of his throat, needing more of him. Needing to connect with him in every possible place. "God, yes. I feel it."

"You're so fucking tight. I need you to come."

I dragged my teeth down his neck, across the tendons. I could almost taste his strength and power. "I'm so close."

Pushing up on his arms, he said, "Touch yourself while I fuck you. Do it now, and do it fast. I can't hold out much longer."

Without an ounce of shame, I followed his instructions. The second I started rubbing my clitoris, I could feel the pressure building inside, a huge wave coming toward me. The intimate touch, combined with Bax's fullness, was too much. I didn't have a hope of withstanding it.

He was watching me, his keen eyes on my face. As he pounded into me, he practically snarled, more animal than man.

I loved it.

His voice was pure wickedness. "That's it. You're my good girl, aren't you, Belle? You're letting me in, so deep inside you. Just me. No other man will ever have you." He started riding me faster, his hips churning. "You're *mine*."

The words took me right over the edge and into the heavens, cast up into the stars and light. A shout ripped from my throat to echo in the room. I held on tight, Bax anchoring me as the muscles in my body convulsed, my walls grasping, pulling him in.

As I started to float down to earth, Bax's hips stuttered, his mouth stretched into a grimace. "Shit, goddamn it. I shouldn't—"

Roaring, he kept pressing and rocking, his eyelids slammed tight. The harsh lines of his face eased in his climax and I loved watching the transformation. This powerful and dangerous man was losing himself in my body, his shaft swelling and pulsing.

It was perfect.

When he slowed, he shook his head. "Just this once. I swear it, Belle."

I pulled him down for a very thorough kiss. "Just once, what?"

"I won't spend inside you again," he said against my mouth. "I couldn't control it this time, but I'll do better next time."

Oh, right. This was how men and women procreated.

My skin heated. I was so foolish. I knew babies resulted from when a man and a woman were in bed together, but I hadn't known exactly how until now. It had taken seeing him spend last night in the handkerchief to having him inside me right now. "You must think I'm silly for not knowing this."

"I could never think you're silly. I blame your father, the women in your life—your entire uptown world—for not teaching you." He kissed me long and hard, our rough exhales mingling as our bodies cooled.

Then he shoved up on his arms and his softened shaft slid from my channel. He moved toward my toes and settled between my legs. I didn't understand what he was doing when he pushed my thighs wider. "Oh, fuck," he whispered as he used one finger to trace my entrance. "There we are. Look at my come mixed with your blood and cream."

After swirling his finger just inside my channel, he lifted it to his mouth and licked the mixture off. His lids fell as his face slackened with pleasure. "Christ almighty."

Then he reached to gather more and held his finger up to my mouth. I didn't hesitate. I opened my lips and let him feed it to me, and the combined taste of us exploded on my tongue. Copper and salt. It was strange, but not bad.

And I liked the idea that it was from the two of us.

A deep groan rumbled out of his chest. "I won't come in you again, I promise."

Then he stood, his thick member hanging down between his legs, and began removing his clothing. No doubt he was trying to distract me from the conversation . . . and it worked. The more he removed, the more fascinated I became with his body. Rough skin stretched over wide shoulders and a broad chest, showing sleek muscles that were not honed in a boxing ring or on the back of a horse. He was pure New York street tough, wiry and strong. A god in silk and wool.

My heart flipped, giddiness filling my lungs—and I froze. What was happening to me? Was I developing feelings for him?

The possibility caused my mouth to dry out. I couldn't. He was Billy Baxter, violent criminal and gang leader. I was . . . the opposite, part of a family who crusaded to bring down the gangs. My father had been trying to rid the city of such ne'er-do-wells for years. There was no future for Bax and me.

"I don't like the expression on your face, widow." Bax shucked off his union suit, leaving him completely bare.

All thoughts in my brain disappeared except for one: *Good heavens, he is gorgeous.* I drank him in slowly. It was my first look at a naked man and I was not going to waste the opportunity. "Turn around."

With a smirk, he spun to show me his backside.

I bit my lip and admired the view. Tall and muscular, he was even more magnificent from this angle. There were scars, signs of the life he'd lived, the fortitude he'd shown to get to the top of the New York City underworld. Perhaps I should've been scared . . . but I wasn't.

Quite the opposite.

He crawled onto the mattress, stretching out his long frame at my side, then cupped my cheek in his palm. His fingers stroked my skin almost reverently. "Thank you for trusting me."

The adoration in his gaze melted my insides, and I couldn't prevent the rush of affection in my chest. "It was perfect, Bax."

"Good." He settled at my side and held me close. "I have an idea."

"Oh?"

"I've been thinking about your undergarments. And the tariffs you talked about."

I studied the far wall and stroked the flat planes of his chest. "Meaning?"

"I can help you skirt the tariffs. If you want to buy more undergarments, that is."

Easing back, I smirked at him. "Why, Bax. Are you encouraging this for my benefit . . . or yours?"

His grin was positively wicked. "Both?"

"So I buy more fancy undergarments and you see me in them, is that it?"

"I call that a win for both sides."

I chuckled. "Rascal." Then I decided to be honest with him. "I once thought of opening a store, where I could sell them publicly. I also have some designs of my own."

"I can help you with that."

"Unfortunately, it's impossible. The daughter of Honest Dan Kelly could never."

"Because you're embarrassed?"

"Because everyone would know I like those undergarments. That I *wear* those undergarments. And besides the tariff problems, Mr. Comstock would probably shut me down over indecency. It's impossible."

"Sweetheart, you can't live your life for other people. If you want to open a store selling racy unmentionables to help women feel pretty and make men want to fuck them, then do it."

He didn't understand. Rules and conventions didn't apply to Bax. "Easy for you to say. You do whatever you like and to hell with the consequences."

"Yes, but I've learned to listen to the only person whose opinion matters: mine."

"Women are not so fortunate. I have to work within the bounds of both society and the law."

"No, you don't. You have me now. I can twist the entire city to suit my whims—and yours. Whatever you want, Belle. You only need to ask."

It was so very tempting. He was offering up my dreams on a silver tray like a glass of champagne. But at what price? What would I need to give up to claim them? My father would never approve. He would rather I stayed inside the house and didn't cause trouble.

I was caught between fantasy and reality, where nothing was quite real.

Bax kissed my forehead. "Think about it."

"I will." Very likely I'd do nothing else. Was it a mistake to turn him down?

Then my breath caught when he began nibbling on my earlobe. "Rest up, yeah? You have five minutes before I make you come again."

CHAPTER 10

Baxter

I waited until she fell asleep before I got up and dressed.

My mind raced over the events of the last few hours. Belle in my bed, Belle begging me to take her virginity. Belle's sweet pussy wrapped around my cock. Jesus fuck, I was a lucky man.

A long-buried part of me had roared to life the second my cock slipped inside her. It had been primal and instinctual, turning me into a snarling beast who would be sated by only one thing: her.

And everything changed in that moment.

I felt the shift deep in my corrupted, jaded soul. She breathed new life into me, like waking me up from a long lonely nap. She was sweetness and joy and unexpected delights, my reward for scrabbling and scratching all these years to survive. I decided right then to keep her.

Belle was mine. I wasn't letting her go, and I'd kill anyone who tried to take her from me.

We could make this work. She was miserable in her uptown

prison, and I could help her spread her wings and fly. More undergarments, her own shop . . . whatever she wanted. I'd give her the fucking world on a gold plate.

Unfortunately, there was the problem of her father. She deserved to know what I did—and why. She needed to learn the truth about Honest Dan Kelly.

I didn't regret kidnapping Kelly. I wouldn't allow the hypocritical blowhard to become mayor. While lining his pockets off blackmail and graft, he campaigned that men like me ruined the city.

Which was ridiculous. Men like me kept Manhattan organized and neat. Without me, crime and lawlessness would run amok here.

Belle would understand. She was a logical, brave woman. I'd explain and show her the proof. She'd soon realize that her father was undeserving of any sympathy or compassion. She would see my side.

And from now on, I would only give her the truth. Her father had lied to her enough.

First, though, I had to deal with her attacker. The piece of shit was found in a Hell's Kitchen alley earlier, shot in the hip. Matty dragged him into the saloon's cellar to stew in fear and misery until I was ready.

After one last look at the woman tucked in my bed, I dragged on my boots and rose. Belle stirred as I crossed the floor. "Bax?"

Her voice was low and thick with sleep, and I longed for nothing more than to crawl back into bed with her. But I needed confirmation about who tried to kidnap her and why. There would be no rest until I killed every last man involved.

"Go back to sleep, sweetheart."

"But where are you going?"

"I have some business I need to handle. I won't be long."

"Promise?"

My chest ballooned at the sweetly-spoken question.

I have to tell her. Soon.

"I promise, widow."

Her sleepy gaze studied my face intently. "Be careful, William."

Before I lost the will to leave, I forced myself out the door. When I entered the cellar, Matty was there, cleaning her nails with a knife, while Charlie stood against the wall with his arms folded. A man lay crumpled on the floor, wheezing. I knew the sound of that wheeze. Belle's attacker wouldn't live much longer.

Using my foot, I rolled him onto his back and waited until pain-filled eyes stared up at me. "Do you know who I am?"

The man's lips moved but no sound emerged. I nudged the bullet wound with the tip of my boot, causing him to howl. When the screams quieted, I snapped, "Answer me."

"Billy . . . Baxter."

"Good. I'm going to ask you some questions and you have two choices. One, you can answer them to my satisfaction and I'll kill you quickly." I bent near the man's face. "Or two, you can refuse to tell me what I want to know and I will peel the skin from your bones. It's your choice.."

The man's eyes were clouded with pain but coherent. He understood the offer. "Don't kill me. I'll tell you anything you want to know."

I dragged over a chair. Then I sat, took out my long knife, and held it loosely in one hand to serve as a reminder. "Who paid you to wait in that building and kidnap her?"

"I-I don't know."

"Wrong answer."

I leaned down, ready to slice, when the man shouted, "Wait!"

I paused and snarled, "Start fucking talking."

"I didn't get his name." Grimacing, he closed his eyes and panted. "But I know he w-works for Walsh."

Exactly as I'd thought. "You said, 'I wonder how much he'll pay to get you back.' Who is 'he'?"

"Ransom her . . . to you."

I nodded. "Where were you supposed to take her?"

"Bank Street."

"The address?"

"Thirty-one."

I glanced at Charlie, who turned on his heel and went up the stairs.

We would find Walsh and this building, and I would have vengeance on every single person involved.

"Is there anything else you can tell me? About the plan, about what Walsh intended?"

"No, sir. I told you all I know."

I rose, removed my coat, and rolled my sleeves high on his forearms while the man on the ground watched, his expression twisted in pain and uncertainty. Then I lifted the chair and placed it against the wall. "You put your hands on her. You scared her. Worst of all, you nearly killed her. For that, I have no mercy. No forgiveness. So I've changed my mind. I won't kill you quickly."

Crouching, I put the tip of the knife directly against the man's balls. "This will be slow. And it will be fucking painful."

For the next hour, the only sounds coming from inside the room were screams.

By the time I finished, I was covered in blood and my body hummed with dark energy. "Dispose of him," I told Matty. "I have to clean up and get back upstairs."

"Have you told her about her father yet?"

I didn't answer. There was a spigot in the cellar with running water, so I used it to wash off. Once I bathed, I put on a clean shirt and trousers, not bothering with a vest and coat in my haste to return to Belle.

As I climbed the stairs, I heard a commotion in the saloon. Damn it. Was there a fight going on? Exhausted and annoyed, I stomped into the main room—and halted.

Belle was there, sitting on top of the wooden bar, laughing with my men, a queen holding court. She was dressed in her gown, her hair piled neatly atop her head, every inch a lady.

My lady.

I grew hot, jealousy building like a frenzy in my blood. I wanted to rip her away from their appreciative gazes and take her back upstairs, keep her just to myself.

"Bax!" She grinned when she saw me. "Come have a drink with us!"

As if they could sense my mood, my men sank lower, hunching, as they slowly turned toward me. My expression had them scurrying off to other parts of the building, leaving Belle alone.

Christ, she was gorgeous, looking at home here in my domain. She fit in perfectly. Unafraid and with no airs whatsoever.

Belle pouted when I reached her. "You made them all leave. We were having fun."

"I bet." Moving in, I touched her jaw, letting my fingers linger on her silky skin. "What are you doing out of bed, widow?"

"I was awake and bored, so I decided to come down. Everyone was very nice to me. I was asking them about you."

No doubt this was true. The men were probably falling all over themselves for her attention by telling stories about me. "Yeah? So what do you think?"

She glanced around, taking in the saloon. "It's nice. Nothing like the rumors."

"The rumors?"

"Things people say. You know, about you. About the gangs. My father—" She sighed and shook her head. "My father tells these stories in his speeches about the gangs and the destruction they cause. Snatching children off the streets to sell to brothels, forcing opium onto unsuspecting women. Murder and violence everywhere they go. But this is nothing like those tales. All the men are . . . sweet."

Sweet, sure. I'd just sliced a man to ribbons one floor below us. But I was glad Belle liked it here. I wanted her by my side for as long as I could keep her.

"You changed your clothes." She ran her hand over my shoulder. "Why?"

I gestured to Asher behind the bar. A half glass of bourbon appeared in front of me, and I downed the liquid in one swallow. *Only the truth from now on.* "We found the man who attacked you and I made him pay. In the process my clothes were soiled."

"Oh."

Our eyes met and I braced myself. I expected to see horror or condemnation.

What I didn't expect to see was *admiration.*

She stared at me like I could do anything, a hero to slay her dragons. I wanted to rip my beating heart out of my chest and place it at her feet. At that moment, there wasn't anything I wouldn't do for her.

And she was beginning to see the truth, how her father had lied about men like me. Now she needed to know everything. It was time.

I jerked my head and Asher disappeared, leaving Belle and me alone at the bar. "There's something we need to discuss."

She trailed her fingers over my chest and down to my stomach. "Does it have to do with returning upstairs?"

I grabbed her hand before she could distract me. "Not yet."

"That's a shame, because I'm not sore any longer."

My cock twitched, pleased at the news, but I ignored it. "It's about what you said. About your father and the stories he tells in his speeches."

She straightened, her eyebrows drawing together. "What about him?"

I paused. I wished I had more time before starting this. My stomach clenched as I searched for the words. "Some crusaders, they don't really believe what they say. But they like the attention it brings, the notoriety that accompanies their words. Often it brings money, as well."

"This doesn't have anything to do with my father, though."

"Yeah, it does, sweetheart. Turns out Honest Dan Kelly ain't so honest after all."

"That's nonsense." She pulled her hand from mine. "The whole city knows of all the good he's achieved in the last seven or eight years."

I plunged ahead. "And there's some of us who know the truth. That he blackmails criminals and lines his pockets through graft and bribery—"

She sucked in a breath, her expression wild with panic. "You're lying. Why would you say these horrible things about my father?"

"I'm not lying, Belle. I have the evidence upstairs. Come with me and I'll show you."

CHAPTER 11

Isabelle

I stared at him, my ears ringing with disbelief. "No, you must be mistaken."

Bax's gaze didn't waver. "He embezzled money from the city. I have the proof."

"Embezzled! He would never do that."

"He did. I can show you the documents up in my office."

This could not be happening. My stomach was churning, squeezing, and I needed Bax to take the words back. "Someone is lying to you, then."

"It's the truth, Belle."

I stared at him, this man who I'd let into my body and my heart. Why was he doing this?

Questions and denials spun like hoops in my brain. "If you have proof of his crimes, why not make it public?"

"I have what I need to ruin him, but we were investigating the boxes of documents we found in his office. We thought there might be more."

His *office?*

I shoved past him and jumped to the floor. Whirling, I put my hands on my hips. "What do you mean, found in his office? Did you have something to do with my father's disappearance?" It hit me like a pile of bricks. "Oh, my God. You lied to me about kidnapping him."

A muscle jumped in his jaw. "Yes, I did. But it was for your own good."

The words fell between us like a stone. Bax had kidnapped my father. I should have known. I never should have believed a criminal over my instincts.

My knees buckled, so I grabbed the smooth wooden bar with one hand to steady myself. "My own good? Tell me, Bax? Why would any of this be good for me?"

"Because he is the worst kind of hypocrite," he snarled. "He's a criminal, like me, but worse because he hides behind fake words and speeches. At least I don't pretend to be anything other than what I am."

"You're trying to *justify* this to me?" I stepped forward and poked his chest. "Where is he? I want him released *right now.*"

His shoulders swelled as his chest expanded. He cast a glance over his shoulder, but I didn't look away. My mind was spinning with fury and disbelief, humiliation and hurt. I wanted to undo this. I wanted to turn back the clock.

I wished I'd never met this man.

Leaning in, I hissed, "I should have shot you when I had the chance."

Without warning, Bax put his shoulder in my belly and lifted me clean off the ground. I pounded his back. "Put me down this instant, Billy Baxter!"

He ignored me. Swiftly, he carried me up the stairs and strode to his apartment. When we were inside, he set me on the floor—and I promptly scrambled away from him. "I want to leave. And I want you to release my father. *Now.*"

He gripped the back of a chair with both hands, his knuckles turning white. "That's not how this works. I decide when your father is released—and I decide when you leave here."

I sucked in a shocked breath. "Is this another kidnapping? Is that what you're doing?"

"I'm not kidnapping you. I'm trying to keep you *safe*. Someone hurt you and tried to kidnap you, Isabelle."

"You already caught and killed that man."

"Which doesn't mean the danger has passed. There's still the man who hired your attacker, yeah?"

"Who is no longer a threat to me after I cease my association with you."

His upper lip curled. "You think ending our *association* will keep you safe? Don't be so naive, widow."

"I know it will! You are the only danger to me in this city, Billy Baxter."

The temperature in the room seemed to drop. His expression turned menacing. Scary. No longer my lover, but the man who ruled the underworld of the city.

He spoke quietly, every word enunciated. "I will lock you up if it keeps you safe, Belle. Even if you hate me for it."

"Oh, so now I am in the wrong? I won't forgive you for this, Baxter. No matter what you do or say. *You kidnapped my father!*"

"He deserves to be ruined, not sit in the mayor's office."

"Then why haven't you ruined him? If that is what you're after, then why not release your proof and sabotage his campaign?"

"I will, when I'm good and ready."

"What's stopping you?" Suddenly, my gaze flicked to the bed. Oh, God. No, no, no. Not that. I put my hand on my stomach, nauseous. "Was this about getting me into your bed? It was, wasn't it? And I fell right into your trap."

"Stop it. I kidnapped your father, but it wasn't like that between you and me."

"Every word out of your mouth has been a lie. I don't believe anything you say anymore."

His expression went blank, his eyes turning hard and flat. "I haven't lied about anything, other than your father's whereabouts."

"Oh, my God. I'm a fool. You were trying to hurt my father by ruining me—and I let you!"

"You have it all wrong, Isabelle."

My laugh was full of bitterness. "No, I'm seeing things clearly for the first time. You are truly horrible. I can't believe I ever had feelings for you."

"We'll discuss this later, after you've sat with it awhile."

"It doesn't matter how long I *sit* with this. I won't forgive you. I'm leaving and I never want to see you again."

His jaw tight, he pointed at me. "I'm not letting you leave until I know you're safe. So wrap your pretty little head around that, while I go and kill every single person involved in hurting you yesterday." He stormed from the room, slammed the door shut, and locked it.

I stared at the door, unable to believe his gall. Bax wasn't letting me go and had *locked me in*. How dare he! Oh, this would not do.

I had to get out of here. I wouldn't meekly await his return, then beg for his attention. No, I'd done enough of that in my lifetime. I was done letting others control me.

I ran to the window. It overlooked the front of the saloon on Forty-Fourth Street. I was too high up to jump and there was no fire escape.

But there was a drain pipe.

A small group appeared on the walk below, with Bax in the lead. He was shouting orders to his men, though his exact words were lost in the wind. I didn't care where he was going or what he was doing. I would never forgive him.

Bax and his guards climbed into a carriage and the wheels started off, while a smaller group loaded into a second vehicle. Betrayal sat in my stomach like a rock, my chest burning with anguish and fury. I should've known better than to trust a man like Billy Baxter.

There would be time for recriminations and regrets later. Right now I needed to escape and find my father.

I opened the window and leaned out. The drain pipe ran the entire length of the building. It was thin, but it should hold. Besides, what choice did I have?

I threw one leg out and adjusted my skirts, trying not to get tangled in the layers of cloth. I reached for the pipe and held on tight, moving slowly out the window until I was completely outside. The metal was wet and slippery, so I dug in, clasping it as hard as I could, using my feet for support. I tried not to look down.

I went slowly, one inch at a time. When my arms began burning, shaking with the effort, I risked a peek at the ground.

It seemed miles away.

Swallowing my fear, I kept going. Finally, I was close enough to jump. My feet landed on the ground with a thud, and I bent over as far as my corset allowed to drag in a deep breath. *God, I hope I never have to do that again.*

I was free.

Now I had to find a hack—

"Going somewhere?"

I whirled around. Matty leaned against the building, one foot propped up on the brick. My stomach plummeted and I began backing away. "W-what are you doing out here?"

"I knew you'd run."

I lowered my chin and raised my fists. "I won't go back inside. You cannot force me."

"You think to fight me?" Matty threw her head back and laughed. "You wouldn't stand a chance, princess."

"I'm tougher than I look."

"I don't doubt it, not if you've hooked Bax."

I hadn't *hooked* Bax—and even if I had, I was throwing him back. "I'm leaving. You can't stop me."

"I don't want to stop you. I want to help you."

This sounded like a trick. "Why?"

Matty pushed off the wall and came closer. "He should've told you about your father. He was a bastard for keeping that from you, which I made perfectly clear many times."

"So, you're going to just let me leave?"

"Yes—and I'm going to tell you where to locate your father." She held out a piece of paper. "There you go."

I snatched the note, but didn't read it. Matty put her fingers in her mouth and let out a piercing whistle. A second later, a hack rounded the corner and stopped in front of us. I stared at the other woman, trying to make sense of it. "I don't understand."

"Then you've never met another woman in dire straits. How nice for you. Not all of us have led a life of such privilege."

I was confused, but I'd never encountered anyone like her. Matty was fascinating and competent. Unafraid and strong. I doubted she'd let a man ever get the best of her.

But I didn't want her to risk herself on my account. "Won't he be angry with you?"

"He'll be spitting mad. But in time he'll come to see I was right. Take this pistol." She held out a gun.

"Thank you."

"I don't need your gratitude. Just promise to help someone else when the time comes." Matty headed toward the saloon doors. "Go in through the rear kitchen. The door's usually unlocked. Go up to the second floor, third door on the right."

I wanted to say thanks again, but Matty disappeared inside the saloon. So I hurried into the hack and gave the driver the address on the piece of paper.

Sadly, it wasn't far, which was both a relief and completely frustrating. This whole time my father had been mere blocks away.

* * *

THE FRONT of the brick townhouse appeared well kept. What was this place? I paid the driver, climbed down and shook out my skirts. Then I moved quickly to the path that ran between the buildings.

Was that laughter I heard inside?

I clasped the butt of my pistol tight in my palm. Were they having a grand time while they tortured my father? I had to hurry.

As Matty predicted, the rear door was unlocked. I slipped inside and found an empty kitchen that smelled of herbs and lemon. Dishes were stacked by the washbasin, waiting to be washed, so I hurried through lest someone come in to begin the task.

A set of servants' stairs led up from the kitchen, so I began to climb. When I reached the second floor I could hear more feminine giggling and the sound of a rhythmic slapping. Wait, was this . . .?

My God. Bax had imprisoned my father in a *bordello*? I ground my back teeth together. My father must be appalled at these conditions. It was exactly the sort of vice and impropriety he railed against in his speeches.

I hurried to the third door on the right. I tried the knob, expecting it to be locked. To my surprise, the door flew open.

I came to an abrupt halt. Naked bodies were sprawled every which way on the bed. Bare limbs filled my vision, and I couldn't piece together what was happening. It was . . . shocking. Confusing. Scandalous.

Then I recognized a face.

My *father's* face.

I couldn't believe it. Dan Kelly was in the midst of it, his hands and mouth quite busy between two women. He didn't appear to be held against his will *at all*.

Heads swiveled toward the door and the coverlet was quickly dragged up to shield the lower half of their bodies. Three surprised faces stared back at me.

Slowly, the coverlet moved and a fourth participant crawled out to peek at me. It was another woman, her big eyes round and wary.

What on *earth*? How did this even work? The silence stretched as I tried to make sense of this *orgy* in front of me.

"Isabelle!" My father scowled as he started to disentangle himself from the bodies. "What are you doing here?"

"Coming to rescue you," I snapped. "But you're clearly in no need of rescuing."

Spinning on my heel, I hurried to the stairs. I was so stupid. I'd climbed out of Bax's saloon and hurried here to rescue my father, anxious to save him from pain and torture.

Except he wasn't suffering at all. He was enjoying himself.

"He is the worst kind of hypocrite. He hides behind fake words and speeches . . . ."

Bax was right. I didn't know my father at all.

"Isabelle," my father called urgently from behind me. "Stop right there."

Taking a deep breath, I whirled on him. Thank heavens he'd put on a dressing gown. "Why? So you can tell me the importance of your work? How you're trying to save the city from corruption and vice? Spare your breath, Papa. I've seen the truth."

"Don't be ridiculous. I am here under duress, yes. But I still have the same needs as other men."

"That was not duress—and this is exactly the sort of thing you've always publicly shamed in your speeches. Houses of sin, you called them. And you've encouraged Comstock and the police to shut them down for years."

"You wouldn't understand, being a sheltered young girl. Someday you'll be married and your husband will teach you about these things." He gave me the same patronizing look he always did when I questioned him. It used to make me feel small; now it made me furious.

I fisted my hands. "Sheltered because you *forced* me to stay home. You said people would use me to get to you. That it was to protect me." I gave a bitter laugh and gestured to the room he'd departed. "Now it's clear you didn't wish for me to discover that you're a hypocrite."

His eyes rounded. "How dare you say such things to me? I am not a hypocrite."

I hadn't ever fought with my father. In all my years I did everything he asked without complaint, thinking he was working toward the greater good. Some greater good, indeed.

Everything Bax had said was true—which I did not find reassuring in the least. No, I felt even more foolish for believing my father for so many years.

But I was done playing the good daughter. I was done pretending like my life didn't matter.

I straightened my spine. "Not a hypocrite, you say? Then I suppose you won't mind when I spread the word of today's orgy, *Honest* Dan Kelly."

"What has come over you?"

Stepping closer, I gave him the truth. "I searched for you for *days*. I went to the police, I went to—" I bit it off, unwilling to say his name. "You have no idea how difficult this has been for me."

"Well, that was foolish. You should have waited at home, as I've taught you. This city is far too dangerous and immoral for the likes of you."

"But just the right sort of immoral for you, apparently."

"Young lady," he growled. "This lack of disrespect will not be tolerated."

"That door wasn't even locked! You could have left at any time. Why didn't you?"

He rolled his shoulders and didn't meet my eye. "I hadn't realized it was unlocked. Obviously I would've left had I known."

Lies. I didn't believe him for one second. I would never believe him—or any other man—as long as I lived. I shook my head. "He tried to tell me what kind of person you are, but I didn't want to hear it. I almost died because of you! What a fool I am."

"Who?" My father grabbed my arm. "Who has filled your head with lies?"

"Let me go," I tried to pull away, but he held tight. "And they weren't lies, it turns out. You are everything he said—and worse."

A deep angry voice reverberated off the walls. "Get your goddamn hands off her, Kelly."

CHAPTER 12

Baxter

I charged up the stairs, a red mist coating my vision. All I could see was Kelly's hand on Belle's arm, and how she was trying to pull away from him.

Kelly sneered at me. "This is none of your concern, Baxter."

"Let Isabelle go immediately," I snarled. "Or I'll rip your arms off, then throw you and your bloody stumps into the East River."

Kelly released her, but didn't move away. "How do you know my daughter's given name?"

Fists clenched, I headed straight for him. "I know more about her than you do, apparently. I know she's under the misguided notion that you're a decent person, that you actually believe the shit you say during those speeches of yours."

Belle shoved past me on her way to the stairs.

"And where are you going?" I asked.

"Go away, Bax."

"Keep Kelly here," I barked at my men as I followed her.

"Leave my daughter alone, you hooligan!" Kelly shouted, leaning over the railing as my men held him back.

I hurried down the stairs. "Fuck off, Kelly."

When I reached the bottom, I caught up to her at the front door. "Widow, wait."

She shook off my hand and whirled toward me. Her face was flushed, her eyes wild. "I'm not a goddamn widow! And I don't want to hear anything you have to say. Ever."

Panic clawed in my throat. I couldn't lose her. I gestured toward the empty drawing room. "I need to talk to you."

"You kidnapped my father, Bax, and you locked me in!"

She tried to edge past me, but I darted into her path. I put my palms up. "I'm not letting you leave until you hear me out. Please, Belle."

I suspected it was the *please* that won her over. She nodded once and marched into the drawing room. "Talk, Bax."

I shoved my hands in my trouser pockets to keep from reaching for her. "I've handled this all wrong."

"Illuminating," she drawled flatly. "And correct."

"Belle, I didn't hurt him. And I wasn't planning to keep him much longer. I just wanted a little more time."

"To dig for more evidence."

"Yes, but also for more time with you."

Her eyes narrowed, like she didn't believe me. "And you feel this justifies lying to me and hurting my family?"

"Does he look hurt?" I pointed to the ceiling. "Let me guess? He's disheveled because he was availing himself of Lisette's hospitality. How many women were there with him?"

"Three—and that is not the point!"

I pressed my palms together, pleading with her. "I know I lied, but I never thought I would develop feelings for you. When I saw you again at the fights, I couldn't help but take advantage of the opportunity."

"What do you mean, when you saw me again?"

Only the truth.

I dragged in a deep breath. "I saw you once outside the mission on Fifty-Second Street. About seven years ago, I suppose. Your father was giving a speech and you were watching him."

She cocked her head. "Seven years ago?"

"Yeah. He called me and some of the other boys vermin. You were with him. I was going to slip a dead rat into his carriage, but then I found you inside."

"I don't recall that."

I wasn't surprised. I would've been another dirty street kid, one of thousands in this city. "I hadn't thought of it in a long time, not until you walked into the fights."

She appeared unimpressed, her mouth flat. I kept talking. "You deserve to escape that big house, Belle. To wear your scandalous undergarments and live the life you want, not the one your father wants. You deserve the truth—and all he did was lie to you."

She wrapped her arms around her waist, as if protecting herself. "Did you think I would fall to your feet in gratitude after you've ruined my father's life? Ruined *my* life? You lied and deceived me."

"No, but I thought you would be reasonable. Don't you see? I want you to stay with me. I want to give you everything."

She gaped at me. "You're from a completely different world than mine. One with kidnappings and lies."

Shame scalded the back of my neck. "There are no different worlds in this city, not like that. The only thing that separates the criminals uptown is their address. Trust me, they're criminals just the same, Belle."

"I'm not a criminal," she hissed. "And my father doesn't *kill* people."

"Oh, so there are some sins you're willing to accept. Just not mine."

"Your flippancy is misplaced. You are perfectly aware of what I mean."

"I hear you making excuses for that bastard upstairs, a man who has ignored you his entire life." I thumped a fist against my chest. "I would lay the entire world at your fucking feet, but you can't forgive me because my sins are somehow greater than Honest Dan Kelly's?"

"If you expect gratitude from me, you'll be waiting until Hell freezes over. I barely know you—and what I do know, I don't like."

I was losing her. She was slipping through my fingers like sand. My voice tightened, fear turning my blood cold. "Horse shit. You know me, almost better than anyone else. And you were happy in the saloon with me and my men. Tell me you didn't love every minute we spent together until you learned about your father's kidnapping."

She blinked several times, her eyes glassy, and I grabbed her hand. "Please, Belle. I will make it up to you."

"You can't. You just want to corrupt me. The perfect uptown princess you can set free and drag downtown into your world. But you don't have the faintest idea of who I am or what I want."

"Wrong. I know you—"

"No you don't, Bax. I'm more than what you *see*. I also have thoughts and feelings. We met *three* days ago, for goodness sake!"

"Then stick around. Give us a chance to get to know each other."

"I'd rather not. I used to trust you. Not anymore, however."

My face fell, the words like a dull knife between the ribs. "Let me change your mind."

"Why must I do all the accommodating when *you* have hurt *me*?"

"I'll make this up to you, I promise."

"It's not enough. My God, you haven't even apologized to me."

"I don't apologize," I said. "Never. Not to anyone."

"Do you hear yourself? You hurt me. You have upended my life, only thinking of yourself. And you won't even apologize for it!"

"Actions are what matter, Belle, not words." After everything with her father, I'd think this was obvious.

She gave a brittle laugh. "The fact that you're not even willing to say it tells me all I need to know."

"Which is?"

"That your pride means more to you than I do."

"Nothing means more to me than you do."

"Except admitting you're sorry, apparently."

I didn't speak. I couldn't. I wasn't sorry. Dan Kelly didn't deserve to be mayor. I would do anything to prevent it.

And I didn't regret a single second of the time Belle and I spent together.

She went around me and headed toward the front entry. "Good-bye, Bax."

I wanted to stop her, take her back to the Devil's Hand and keep her with me forever. But I couldn't kidnap her. I called, "This isn't over."

"I'm terribly *sorry*," she drawled with a heavy dose of mockery. "But this is most definitely over."

"Someone could still try to hurt you."

She paused with her hand on the doorknob. "Did you handle the man responsible for my kidnapping attempt?"

"Yes, Walsh is dead." We'd found Walsh in New Jersey. I'd killed him quickly, eager to get back to Manhattan. "But—"

"Then we needn't worry. Besides, no one on earth could possibly hurt me more than you have, Billy Baxter." She yanked open the door and disappeared outside.

Sucking in a ragged breath, I stared at the wood floor. The walls closed in as my stomach sank to my toes.

Shit. I'd lost her.

CHAPTER 13

Baxter

Once again, I broke into Daniel Kelly's office after dark.

While the breaking in part felt familiar, everything else was different.

It all changed after Belle's departure, from the way I looked at myself to the way I saw the world.

And I didn't like what I discovered. She was right. I'd let my pride and feelings for her father cloud my judgment. I took away her choices and backed her into an impossible corner.

I deserved to lose her.

And so, for the first time in my life, I was doing the right thing. The decent thing. It wouldn't get her back, but not doing it would hurt her. And I would do everything in my power to keep Belle from hurting ever again.

Easing the window open, I threw a leg over the sill and climbed inside.

Daniel Kelly was at his desk, a lamp turned low in the corner. The soft glow illuminated the pistol in his hand.

"I ought to shoot you," he snarled. "How dare you come here, Baxter?"

Four days ago I released him. Four days since Isabelle walked out of my life. She hated me—and I didn't blame her.

I waved my hand at Kelly's gun. "Put that down and hear me out."

"You'd like that, wouldn't you?" His lips twisted into a sneer. "So you can kidnap me again. Go to hell!"

Already there.

I dropped into the arm chair across from his desk. "You're going to want to hear what I have to say."

"What I want is to shoot you right between the eyes." He leaned in, the gun never wavering. "You seduced *my daughter*, you filthy piece of—"

"Stop." I held up my hand. "Calling me names got you into this mess in the first place. I suggest you keep a civil tongue in your head."

"Are you denying you seduced her?"

I thought of Belle, throwing her leg over my hips and begging me to fuck her. *"I know what kind of man you are, and I know how you feel about me. This feels right to me, here and now."*

But she hadn't really known me or what I was capable of.

And the hatred and disappointment in her eyes when she finally did learn?

It haunted me. I couldn't breathe, couldn't *think* without her. I'd hurt her—and I hated myself for it.

"I seduced her," I admitted. "And you can shoot me for it, if you want. But I'd suggest waiting to hear me out first."

"Why? So you can attempt to justify it?" He gave a bitter laugh. "I know the reason. You did it to hurt and humiliate me!"

I shook my head. "Wrong. It was about her. And I'd do it all over again if I had the chance."

He hadn't expected that, if his bewildered expression was anything to go by. "You're full of shit."

"You don't know a damn thing about your daughter, do you? She's

. . . ." I swallowed the lump in my throat. "Perfect. She's brave and kind, loyal and caring. She would've gone to the ends of the earth to save your corrupt ass."

"Yes, she told me about holding a gun on you at the fights. If only she'd shot you then, it would have saved us all a great deal of aggravation."

"No doubt. But then the evidence I had would have reached the newspapers."

"Had? Don't tell me you've destroyed it, because I won't believe you."

"No, I gave it to your daughter."

I left the papers proving Kelly's misdeeds in Belle's bedchamber just before crawling in to the office. She'd been downstairs at supper, ignoring her father while she ate.

"You gave it all to Isabelle? Why on earth would you do that?"

"Because she deserves to know the real Honest Dan Kelly."

"Jesus Christ," he muttered before his jaw hardened. "So this is where you blackmail me, I suppose? It's exactly what I'd expect from someone like you."

"Vermin, you mean?" I fisted my hands but tried to remain calm. "I'm not here to blackmail you."

"Why not?"

"Because exposing you would hurt her."

He cocked his head, like he was trying to hear better. "Let me understand. You were willing to do anything to prevent me from becoming mayor—even kidnapping me—but you're giving up because you believe it will upset my daughter?"

"I *know* it will upset your daughter. She stupidly loves you. And don't pretend like you didn't fuck your way through that bordello. I asked Lisette."

He didn't say anything, not that I expected him to.

Slapping my hands on my thighs, I pushed to my feet. "Well, that's that. Best of luck in robbing the fine citizens of this city."

He also stood, not lowering the gun for an instant. "It's no different than what you do, Baxter."

"True. But I've never claimed otherwise. I'm a villain, through and through. You pretend to be a savior, but you're just as bad, yeah?"

His nostrils flared, but he didn't comment on that. Instead, he said, "I won't let you have her, even if I have to kill you to prevent it."

A bitter bark of laughter escaped my throat. "You keep her locked in this house, isolated and alone. But you can't control her. She has her own mind, her own goals. A word of advice? Don't try to get in her way. Because she'll only hate you for it."

"I don't need tips from you on how to raise my daughter. And a word of advice from *me*? Stay away from her. If I catch you near her again, I will shoot you, Baxter."

"You can try, Kelly, but I love her. I'm not giving up, not until she hears me out."

The other man sneered. "Is she worth dying over?"

"Yes."

The door flew open. I turned—and found Belle there. My body jolted, and I couldn't look away. I drank in the sight of her, mesmerizing every detail. Her hair was pulled into a simple braid, and bare feet peeked out from under her dressing gown.

Christ, she was lovely. My fierce widow.

My chest felt hollow, like a fist was squeezing my heart. I needed to say something. I needed to beg for her forgiveness, pledge my undying love. Let her hear how goddamn sorry I was.

Just as I opened my mouth, the gun went off. All the air left my lungs as pain exploded in my body. My legs went out from under me and I was on the ground, staring at the ceiling. The last thing I saw was Belle's panicked face. I had so much I wanted to tell her . . . then everything went black.

CHAPTER 14

Isabelle

$\mathcal{B}$ax wouldn't wake up.

I hovered near his bedside, unwilling to leave. The doctor had removed the bullet two days ago, but Bax developed a fever shortly after. He'd thrashed and muttered, tortured by what sounded like childhood memories of torment and pain. My heart had ached for him as I struggled to keep him alive.

I forced water and broth down his throat. Bathed him in a cool cloth when the fever spiked, covered him when he shivered. Matty helped, but I did most of it by myself.

I would not let this man die.

Seeing my father shoot Bax in the back had been the most terrifying moment of my life. My scream brought Matty and two of Bax's men charging into my home. My father's face was deathly pale, like he couldn't believe he'd actually pulled the trigger, but no one paid him any attention. Not with Bax unconscious and bleeding on the floor.

We loaded Bax into his carriage, while one of the men raced to fetch the doctor. I held Bax's head in my lap as Matty pressed on his wound with a cloth, trying to stem the blood.

Bax's life dangled by a thread in those next few hours, and I vowed not to leave until he was better.

Finally the fever broke, and there was nothing to do but wait. I kept myself busy by listing my grievances toward him. Even though he couldn't hear me, it helped. I was still furious with him.

I must've fallen asleep because the softest brush of a fingertip across my cheek startled me awake. Where was I?

I straightened, memory rushing back. My eyes flew to his face—and I found him staring up at me. "Bax," I breathed, my chest expanding with relief. It was so good to see his sharp gaze once more.

"I'm sorry," he croaked.

An apology? I never thought to hear those words out of his mouth. Was he delirious? I felt his forehead. He was cool to the touch. "Please rest. You needn't talk right now."

He frowned and weakly gripped my hand. "I'm sorry, Belle."

"Bax, you nearly died. Do not overexert yourself."

"I'm sorry."

I bit my lip, torn between amusement and frustration. Then I reached for the water glass I had by his bed and helped him take a sip.

"I'm sorry," he repeated as I replaced the glass.

"You plan on continuing, I assume, until I acknowledge your apology."

"I'm—"

"Baxter!" I threw my hands up and let them fall in my lap. "Stop it. I hear you. Let me check your bandages."

I rose and leaned over the bed. Just as I peeled back his bandages to ensure the wound wasn't infected, he said, "Forgive me."

The hole was healing nicely, packed with some medicinal herbs that Matty swore worked on almost any injury. I replaced the bandage and sat down. "I appreciate the apology."

"Wanted to tell you . . . at your house. Before I was shot."

Two days, but it felt like a lifetime. "I heard you tell my father you love me." And that I was worth dying for, which couldn't be true. Yet he'd turned his back on his enemy, knowing there was a loaded pistol trained on him. "You also gave me the evidence you collected. I cannot believe you relented after all this time."

"I would . . . do anything for you."

"Just because you didn't ruin him doesn't mean you are absolved of wrong-doing."

"I'm sorry."

"Oh, sakes alive." I pushed off the chair and started pacing. "Don't say it again. It won't make any difference. I can't forgive you."

He struggled to sit up and winced. I rushed over and helped him back down to the mattress. "Stay still or else you'll reopen that wound."

"Have to . . . make you listen." Sweat dotted his forehead, his breath labored. "Please."

"I'm listening." I wiped his brow with a cool cloth. "I heard almost every word you said to my father."

"Belle, I need you."

Was he in pain? Uncomfortable? Hungry? I swept a lock of his hair off his face with my fingertips. "What is it? Do you need laudanum? Broth?"

"No, I need *you*. Here. Always."

My chest ached. Hurt and confusion battled with happiness over his declaration. And a big part of me wanted to stay. I loved this man, and nearly losing him showed me how precious our time was here on this Earth.

But I couldn't.

I had to decide what I wanted in life. Not what my father wanted or what Bax wanted. This was about *me*.

Nearly my whole existence had been spent alone, locked away. And both of the men I'd trusted had let me down. I couldn't rely on my judgment, clearly. I had to stand on my own, gain life experience, before attempting to trust anyone ever again.

"I can't." I choked out the words and stepped away from the bed.

His fingers fisted the coverlet, his body tensing. "Don't go. Please."

My heart squeezed. The agony in his expression shredded my

insides, but I knew I was doing the right thing. I couldn't stay. And it was probably better to leave now, while he was still too weak to stop me.

A cowardly move, but Bax had a habit of kidnapping people.

I drank in his rough, beautiful features for the last time. No man would ever mean more to me. And though I was angry with him, I was also grateful. He'd shown me so much in our short time together.

Stepping closer, I bent and pressed my lips to his forehead. "Thank you. Because of you I want more for myself. Now I just need to figure out what *more* means."

He tried to grab my arm but didn't have the strength. "No, Belle. I can help."

"I don't want your help." Perhaps a tad harsh, but the words were true. "I have to do this on my own."

I could see the moment he shut me out. It was like a curtain descended over his expression. One second he was staring at me eagerly, desperately. Then his gaze became impersonal, with no hint of emotion. As if I were an inanimate object, like a piece of dust or a plant.

Then he shifted his head, looking away.

My hands shook with the need to touch him, but I kept perfectly still. This was for the best. Bax was going to live. He would continue his reign here in Hell's Kitchen, while I figured out the rest of my life. Perhaps our paths would cross again one day.

If only it didn't hurt so much.

Tongue thick, I whispered, "Be well, William."

He didn't acknowledge me, didn't even blink.

So I left.

On my way down the steps, I passed Matty. Whatever she saw in my face had her straightening off the wall. I licked my lips to moisten them. "He's awake. Fever's gone."

"You coming back?"

The backs of my eyelids burned as I shook my head. "Take care of him for me."

She squeezed my shoulder briefly before letting her hand drop. "I always do. You need anything, you know how to find me. And it can stay quiet."

I never expected such kindness from her, and I nearly started crying right then. "Thank you."

She went up the stairs toward the man I loved and I walked in the opposite direction. Toward the street.

Toward my uncertain future.

CHAPTER 15

Isabelle

Three months later

It was strange to be on my own. Strange, but also exhilarating. My father and I hadn't spoken since I moved out of our Upper East Side home. I lived above my shop these days, and I loved it.

My shop.

Hard to believe, but the place was really mine. After fencing my jewelry, I had enough money to buy a small storefront and adjoining apartment. Then I put both parts of my plan into motion.

First, I approached a few modistes and asked them to let me sell some of their undergarments on consignment. As dresses were their true money items, most of them readily agreed to supply me with corsets, drawers, silk stockings, and the like. This gave me the inventory to open up the doors.

The second part of my plan would take a bit longer. When I had extra money, I would take my own designs back to the modistes and pay to have them made. These pieces would have a label under the store's own name: *Belle's.*

We were an instant success. I chose a space near both Ladies' Mile and the Tenderloin district, which gave me a wide clientele. Curious and daring uptown ladies shopped here, as well as flocks of dancers and actresses. And the working girls of the bordellos were some of our best customers.

Though I was busy, I still had time to think about Bax.

Had he moved on without me? Of course he had. Did I honestly think Billy Baxter was pining away for me? I didn't dare ask Matty when she occasionally stopped by to visit.

Regardless, it felt as if something was missing from my life. Or rather, someone. I just wasn't sure what to do about it.

Could I forgive him? I didn't know. As time went on, I wasn't as angry. Just hurt.

"No, I need you. Here. Always."

My lungs constricted and I pressed a hand to my chest. Sakes alive, I ached for him.

The bell above the door chimed and I left my office in the back to come out front. Matty was there, her expression flat and angry.

"Hello, Matty," I called.

She didn't greet me. Instead, she slapped a piece of paper on the counter. "You broke him."

My jaw fell, but I quickly recovered. "What are you talking about?"

"You fucking broke him, Belle. And I need you to fix him." She pushed the paper over. "Look at that."

I looked down and almost swallowed my tongue. "This can't be real."

"Oh, it's real. He's out on the campaign trail already."

I studied the advertisement, which was a very gentlemanly portrait of one William Baxter, candidate for the position of mayor. Of New York City.

I couldn't help it—I laughed. "This is absurd. He'll never get elected."

"You know who he's running against, yeah?"

My amusement died. Dan Kelly was the current front-runner in the mayoral election. I still possessed the evidence against my father, but I hadn't released it on the condition that he left the gangs alone. "Why is Bax doing this?"

"To win you back. To be worthy of you."

I locked eyes with her. Matty was deadly serious, unhappiness etched in the lines of her face. "That doesn't make any sense."

"He hasn't said as much, but I know what's going through his thick head. Belle, this"—she pointed to the paper—"is going to ruin everything and likely get us all killed."

I knew the gangs were territorial. Any sign of weakness was seen as an invitation for enemies to attack. "Is there a chance you're exaggerating?"

"No. The other gangs won't allow Bax to ascend to fucking royalty. It's one thing to have a politician or two in your pocket. It's another to have all the pockets and all the politicians at your disposal."

It would be unprecedented power in the city. Bax would control not only the underworld, but the political world, as well.

"Shit," I muttered.

That got her lips to twitch. "You've really taken to cursing in these last few months. I approve."

I shoved the paper toward her. "I don't know what you expect me to do."

"You have to talk to him. Convince him this is a bad idea. Take him back. Kiss and make up." She lifted the paper and shook it. "Because he will die if he pursues this."

"You say take him back as if that's an easy decision."

Bending, Matty rested her elbows on the counter. "Please. You named the place Belle's, after all. Those dark circles under your eyes haven't let up, even when the store started to turn a profit. You've lost at least fifteen pounds. Maybe more, the way your dresses hang off you. When will you admit you miss him, for Christ's sake?"

Damn. Why must this woman be so perceptive?

I lifted my shoulders. "If he won't listen to you, then he certainly won't listen to me."

"Wrong. You're the only person who convince him he's worthy exactly as he is."

"I don't see how—"

"He's miserable and he loves you," she repeated softly. "This is a last-ditch effort to win you back. Even if it's just to tell him it won't work, go and talk to him, please."

Was I ready to see him? A strange flutter erupted behind my sternum. I was still angry with him, of course, but the idea of losing Bax was intolerable. It would destroy me if something bad happened to him.

Because I'm still in love with him.

I ignored that inner voice, the one getting louder and louder by the day. But this wasn't about a future with Bax. This was about keeping him from making a huge mistake.

And I had to find a way to make him listen.

An idea came to me then. A very wicked idea. I grinned at Matty, the first real smile I'd given in months. "I need your help."

* * *

Baxter

I CAME AWAKE SLOWLY, my mind filled with cotton. Had I been shot again? I remembered leaving the campaign office last night—

Shit! I'd been jumped from behind by four or five men and forced into a carriage. They must've drugged me, because everything else was a fog.

I tried to move, but my arms and legs were held tight. I was trapped, tied to a chair. I tried to stay calm. Panicking never solved a damn thing. Where the fuck was I?

The room was dark, with no windows to offer light of any kind. I squinted, trying to see if someone was there. When I got loose I would beat every one of these sons of bitches to death.

Twisting my wrists, I tried to get free. I gritted my teeth as the rope dug into my skin. Goddamn it. These were tied with no give whatsoever. Matty was the only person I knew who could tie ropes so well.

The door opened and the light switched on. I blinked, unable to see. "I'm gonna to get free and slice you into little pieces," I growled at the shadowy figure by the door.

"I certainly hope not."

I froze, my heart leaping into my throat. That voice. It couldn't be.

My eyes finally adjusted. It was her. *Isabelle.*

God almighty, she was gorgeous. A navy dress hugged her curves, soft wisps of blond hair framing her face. My tongue dried out as her gaze locked with mine. I felt the impact of those blue eyes down to my toes.

"Hello, Bax."

The sound of her voice hollowed out my stomach. "Isabelle."

She folded her arms across her chest and cocked her head. "Tell me why."

"Why what?"

"Why you're running for mayor."

I hadn't seen her in months and this was what she wished to discuss? "As soon as you tell me why you've kidnapped me and tied me to a chair."

"I want to know why, Bax."

"Why not?" I shrugged as best as I could, being tied to a chair and all. "If your father can do it, anyone certainly can."

"He's been a city employee for years. And as far as Manhattan is concerned, he has a sterling reputation."

"You think I won't win."

"I think you're trying to prove something."

"Sure." I huffed a dry laugh. "That I have enough money for campaign bribes."

"Bax," she sighed and closed the distance between us. "We both know you're trying to prove you're good enough."

My back stiffened. "I don't need to prove a damn thing." A lie, but I'd never admit it.

Now she was before me, and it was the worst kind of torture to have her this close and not be able to touch her. "Are you going to untie me now?"

"No, not until you come to your senses."

I didn't wish to discuss politics with her. I'd missed her so fucking much. I studied the delicate features of her face. I knew every freckle, every curve. She looked thinner, but still beautiful.

"There's no reason to run for mayor," she continued. "You don't need to prove anything to the world. Look at how far you've come."

And it still wasn't enough to keep her.

"There's always higher to climb," I said.

"Running for mayor will get you killed."

I inhaled, trying to catch a hint of her sweet scent. "Probably."

"I can't let you do that."

"Why?"

I waited for her to say more, but the silence stretched. My heart fell.

It wasn't enough. She didn't love me or want to stay with me. And why would she? Our past could never be undone—and that was my fault.

Clenching my jaw, I struggled uselessly against the bindings. *Matty and her fucking knots.* "I appreciate your concern. I'll be fine. Now, untie me."

"Do not dare get angry with me, William. You have no right whatsoever."

I could feel my protective walls crumbling, all the built-up anger and misery leaking out. "I confessed my love and apologized. I begged you to stay. And you left!"

She pointed her finger at me. "You know why I left. You kidnapped my father. You lied to me." She drew in a deep breath and let it out. "You hurt me."

"And I'm fucking sorry for that, Isabelle. So damn much. I know you'll never be able to forgive me—and it rips my heart out, woman."

"Oh, Bax." She sighed heavily. "In some ways, I'm grateful."

I wasn't sure I heard right. "Grateful?"

"I was living a lie. I thought my father was a paragon, a crusader who would change the city. It made his ignoring me easier to tolerate. I accepted it, did whatever he said. I was the perfect daughter."

"You're still perfect," I pointed out.

Her expression softened. "There was once a princess, locked in a tower. She lived a lonely life until a brave knight came to set her free. He gave her the gift of independence."

Her skirts brushed the tips of my shoes as she leaned in and placed her palms on my bound chest. What was happening? I licked my lips, the need for her swelling, clawing inside me. "The knight didn't do that. The princess did it all on her own."

"Well, he helped. And do not disparage the man I fell in love with."

My heart tripped over itself. "Love?"

"Love," she confirmed with a nod of her head. "I fell in love with a gangster. But he's more than just a thug. He's loyal and smart, so very brave. And he would do anything for me."

"Absolutely anything. Just fucking ask, sweetheart."

"Drop out of this silly mayoral race."

"Done. Now, untie me." I needed to touch her in the worst way.

Instead, she bit her lip and slid onto my lap. My body instantly responded to the feel of her soft curves.

Her fingers tangled in my hair. "That was easy. And here I thought you wouldn't listen. I was worried that you'd moved on."

Was she cracked? The words tumbled from my mouth. "There is no moving on from you, widow. I'm drowning without you, but I can't feel it. I can't feel anything."

"I miss you, too. Very much."

I forced the words out, though I feared I might be wrong. "Does this mean you're giving me another chance?"

She rested her forehead against my jaw. "Are your kidnapping days behind you?"

"When it comes to you and your family, yes."

She threw her head back and laughed. "You're impossible."

"If you're hoping to redeem me, I will disappoint you."

"I don't want to redeem you, William. I want to love you."

Jesus, those were the sweetest words I'd ever heard. I kissed her temple. "Oh sweetheart. I'm going to spend the rest of my life making you happy. Every day. You'll never regret it."

She hummed and shifted on my lap. The friction sent fresh waves of sparks through my blood. She said, "I wish you had been honest with me from the start."

"From now on, I will be."

"You'd best mind that promise, Bax. Because I really will shoot you this time if you don't."

I couldn't help but grin. My bloodthirsty girl. "I hope you do."

She patted my chest. "Then this means I'm yours and you're mine."

"And you'll come live with me in Hell's Kitchen, yeah?"

"Eventually." She ran a finger along my jaw. I shivered, the light touch driving me out of my skull.

"Untie me, widow. Right the fuck now."

"I don't think so. I like having you at my mercy."

"I need to get my hands on you. Please, Belle."

"I'd much rather show you the undergarments I wore just for you."

More blood rushed between my legs, and my cock went rigid. I couldn't move, and yet I liked this game we were playing.

I put my lips close to her ear. "You gonna be a good girl for me and put on a show?"

"Let's call it research for the store, shall we?" Climbing off my lap, she moved to stand in front of me. "Would you like to see the drawers or the corset first?"

"The drawers," I instantly answered.

"Then I think I'll start with the corset."

I groaned and closed my eyes. "You brought me here to torture me."

"Indeed, I did. It's nothing less than you deserve. Watch carefully, darling."

The endearment caught me by surprise, the result like an electric charge to my blood. "Goddamn it. Hurry, woman."

She unfastened her bodice slowly, methodically, and I clenched my teeth to keep from snarling at her to go faster. I was dying for her. Starving. I didn't know how much more I could take. By the time her bare arms emerged, I was breathing hard.

The corset cover was pale pink, a delicate scrap of nearly transparent fabric. She removed it like she had all the time in the world, the vixen.

"Belle," I snarled.

"Patience, William."

She placed the cover on the chair, where the bodice rested. When she stood, I got a look at the corset. Black silk edged in pink, the dark fabric a perfect contrast to her milky skin. Her tits were pressed high and tight, begging for my mouth.

"*Fuuuck.*" I groaned and tried to free myself once more.

Her lips twisted with a secret smile as her fingers started on the ties of her skirts. I wasn't going to last through all the layers. It was awful, sitting here watching when I could be touching her.

I could torture her, too.

"I love you so much, sweetheart," I said in a low, seductive tone. "I'm going to make you so goddamn happy. Every morning I'll wake you up with my mouth between your legs, feasting on your pussy. You like that, don't you? When I tongue your cunt?"

She exhaled shakily and the ties in her fingers knotted. She quickly got them undone. "Stop distracting me."

I didn't miss how fast she was breathing, the flush to her skin. "Then, after you come, I'll slide my cock inside you a little at a time. So you can really feel it, yeah?"

The outer skirt fell to the floor. She moved faster on the petticoat. *Good.*

I kept up a stream of erotic conversation until she was down to her drawers. Black, just like the corset. Just like my soul. Yeah, she would fit in fine with me in Hell's Kitchen.

"Get over here," I growled.

"Do you like them?"

"I fucking love them. They're perfect, just like you." I rolled my wrists again, trying to get free. "Now, come straddle my lap and take out my cock, Belle. I want to show you how much I missed you."

She bit her lip and came toward me, her tops of breasts bouncing above the corset. "You are quite bossy for a man who broke my heart."

Guilt lanced through me. "I'm sorry, sweetheart. You can torture me as long as you want."

"That's better." Now standing before me, she slipped her fingers into the slit of her drawers.

Then she rubbed herself and moaned.

My mouth fell open. *Christ.* She really was going to torture me.

Her lids fell closed. "Every time I did this I thought of you."

I couldn't do this. I wasn't strong enough. Writhing against the ropes, I begged, "Have mercy on me, widow. I'm dying here. For God's sake, please."

"You'll never lie to me again?"

"No, I swear it."

She kept circling her clit. "And you won't get shot again?"

"I'll do my best, sweetheart."

"Good, because I have no wish to become a true widow."

I froze. Was she saying . . .?

I licked my lips. "I want to marry you. I want you at my side every second of every day. You are the air I breathe and the blood in my veins. I'll spend my life giving you the fucking world, if you let me."

Expression softening, she came over to stand mere inches away. She slipped her fingers into my mouth, the same fingers that had been stroking her clit. The musky flavor of her pussy flooded my senses and I moaned, sucking on her skin. My God, this woman.

"I don't need the world," she whispered, taking her fingers away. "I just need you." She threw one leg over my lap.

"You have me, sweetheart. Now fuck me and put me out of my misery, yeah?"

* * *

Thank you for reading *The Gangster's Prize*!

If you like your historical romance short and spicy, check out MY DIRTY DUKE, my age-gap bang-fest!

* * *

Violet knows that her father's best friend, the Duke of Ravensthorpe, is the most powerful man in all of London with a reputation for sin.

But nothing can stop Violet from wanting to shed her wallflower ways and fulfill her darkest, most forbidden desires…even if it means seducing a man twice her age.

"Shupe is a true queen of filth, expert at spinning heartfelt love stories alongside tantalizingly wicked scenarios."
—*Entertainment Weekly*

Click here to read *My Dirty Duke*
for FREE in Kindle Unlimited or buy the eBook direct on Amazon.

Fifth Avenue Rebels:

The Heiress Hunt

The Lady Gets Lucky

The Bride Goes Rogue

The Duke Gets Even

The Uptown Girls:

The Rogue of Fifth Avenue

The Prince of Broadway

The Devil of Downtown

The Four Hundred Series:

A Daring Arrangement

A Scandalous Deal

A Notorious Vow

The Knickerbocker Club:

Tycoon

Magnate

Baron

Mogul

Wicked Deceptions:

The Courtesan Duchess

The Harlot Countess

The Lady Hellion

Novellas:

My Dirty Duke

Sold to the Duke

How The Dukes Stole Christmas Anthology

Miracle on Ladies' Mile

AUTHOR'S NOTE

Thanks for reading *The Gangter's Prize,* my Gilded Age take on Thomas Shelby. (IYKYK.) I hope you enjoyed it!

This story was originally published in the Villain I'd Like to F… anthology, which was the third super-spicy historical anthology I did with Sierra Simone, Adriana Herrera, Eva Leigh and Nicola Davidson. Please check out their work, because they are amazing writers with super-spicy steam.

The Gangster's Prize is a little different because it's in 1st person point of view. I know that's not every reader's cup of tea, but sometimes with a villain you need to be inside their head to really like (and root for!) the character. I hope you liked Bax.

Now my research notes!

The scandal with Caroline Astor's gowns is true.

Lyon really was the center of Europe's silk industry.

Isabelle's father, "Honest" Dan Kelly, is based on "Honest John" Kelly, a Tammany Hall leader and U.S. Representative in New York in the late 1800s.

If you're looking for more history on French lingerie in the late 19th-century, author Geri Walton has this great piece on her blog.

For more tidbits and historical factoids, join my newsletter, The Gilded News.

ABOUT THE AUTHOR

USA Today bestselling author **Joanna Shupe** has always loved history, ever since she saw her first Schoolhouse Rock cartoon. Since 2015, her books have appeared on numerous yearly "best of" lists, including *Publishers Weekly*, *The Washington Post*, *Kirkus Reviews*, Kobo, and BookPage.

Sign up for Joanna's Gilded Lilies Newsletter for book news, sneak peeks, reading recommendations, historical tidbits, and more!

www.joannashupe.com